She was completely naked

Jeremy's heart slammed hard against his ribs as he watched the tall, slender woman climb onto a rock by the lake. He held his breath until he thought his lungs would burst. When he finally breathed, Anna dove back into the river.

He fought against the sensations that seemed to hit him with the force of a lightning bolt. He was a man who loved women, and he was always aware of their beauty.

But he'd never had a reaction like the one Anna had just evoked.

He had to get control of himself and the situation. His future depended on it.

During the long, hot hours of tracking her, he'd anticipated all kinds of trouble. He hadn't thought of this. Now all he wanted to do was kiss her—run his hands all over that wet skin....

Dear Harlequin Intrigue Reader,

Chills run down your spine, your pulse pounds...and you can't wait to turn the page! It's just another month of outstanding romantic suspense from Harlequin Intrigue.

Last month, Amanda Stevens introduced you to a new brand of justice—GALLAGHER JUSTICE—in *The Littlest Witness* (#549). This month, Detective Tony Gallagher gets his very own *Secret Admirer* (#553) for Valentine's Day. Cupid is also hard at work in B.J. Daniels's *Love at First Sight* (#555), in which a sexy police officer has to pose as the husband of the only witness to a murder in order to protect her. Except he keeps forgetting their marriage is supposed to be a façade.

Caroline Burnes takes a break from her FEAR FAMILIAR series to bring you *Texas Midnight* (#554). Simmering passion and a remote location make for an explosive read from this bestselling author. But Familiar, the crime-solving black cat, will be back at Harlequin Intrigue soon in his *thirteenth* novel! Watch for *Familiar Obsession* (#570) in stores this June.

Finally, Rita Herron contributes to the ongoing Harlequin Intrigue amnesia promotion A MEMORY AWAY... with *Forgotten Lullaby* (#556). In this highly emotional story, not only do a man and woman commit their love to one another once, but they also overcome the odds to fall in love all over again.

Intense drama and powerful romance make for an extraspecial selection of titles this February. Enjoy!

Sincerely,

Denise O'Sullivan
Associate Senior Editor
Harlequin Intrigue

Texas Midnight
Caroline Burnes

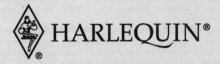

HARLEQUIN®

TORONTO · NEW YORK · LONDON
AMSTERDAM · PARIS · SYDNEY · HAMBURG
STOCKHOLM · ATHENS · TOKYO · MILAN · MADRID
PRAGUE · WARSAW · BUDAPEST · AUCKLAND

ISBN 0-373-22554-7

TEXAS MIDNIGHT

Copyright © 2000 by Carolyn Haines

This edition published by arrangement with Harlequin Books S.A.

® and TM are trademarks of the publisher. Trademarks indicated with
® are registered in the United States Patent and Trademark Office, the
Canadian Trade Marks Office and in other countries.

Visit us at www.romance.net

Printed in U.S.A.

ABOUT THE AUTHOR

Caroline Burnes is currently involved in writing her books and "gentling" her three-year-old Connemara/Thoroughbred gelding, Cogar. An animal advocate, she believes that kindness and consistency are the keys to relating to animals—big or little. She also has two mares, three dogs and six cats.

Books by Caroline Burnes

*Fear Familiar

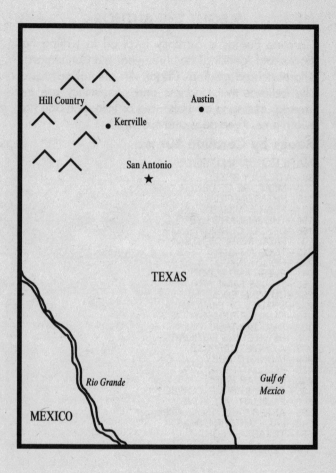

CAST OF CHARACTERS

Anna Red Shoes —Her unthinking actions put her on the run with a man she's sworn to hate, but is coming to love.

Jeremy Masterson —He started the hunt for Anna—now he just wants to keep her safe.

Ellie Clark —The bookstore owner is Jeremy's oldest friend and supporter.

Lucinda Estar —She's glamorous, spoiled—and deadly?

Blane Griffin —His friendship with Jeremy has turned to wild jealousy.

Maria Gonzalez —How high might she price her friendship with Anna?

Henry Mills —Someone literally stabbed the editor in the back.

Johnny Severe —Does he want Anna back, or does he want to destroy her?

Gabriel Wexit —She charmed her way into Jeremy's life. What does she really want?

To the Ellen Drive gang—especially Rat Boy
Tommy Beech and the cowgirl Rat-ettes.
They can't sing, but they can ride.

Chapter One

Jeremy Masterson leaned back in his chair and made eye contact with the pretty little brunette who was smiling at him from the back of the audience. She looked to be about thirty and ripe for the picking. And she was hanging on every word he spoke. Yes indeed, life was good.

He closed the book he'd read a brief passage from and noticed Ellie Clark, the bookstore owner, giving him a look that signaled a large dose of warning. Ellie was no dummy, and she'd picked up on the little flirtation he'd started with the brunette. *Ah, Ellie.* She was his best friend and his conscience, but he was ready for a celebration. And he didn't want to party alone.

Ellie came to stand beside him. She placed a hand on his shoulder. ''Jeremy will sign books over at the table. Please help yourself to some wine and refreshments,'' she said, putting an official end to the reading.

''I want to thank all of you for coming,'' Jeremy added, taking Ellie's cue. It was time to quit flirting and start signing. There were about a hundred people in the audience, and it would take some time to meet, greet and sign for each one. He couldn't help a grin of self-satisfaction. *Blood on the Moon,* his novel about the settling of his home state of Texas, had finally put him on the way to fame and fortune. It had been a long, hard road.

Ellie leaned down. "Henry called from your ranch. He's having some problems with the new book."

Jeremy forgot about the book signing and the brunette as he looked up into Ellie's worried blue eyes. "He said not to worry you. He was rechecking some of the facts about the Indian raids after 1875. Since *Blood on the Moon* has gotten so much notice, he said it was vital that there weren't any mistakes in the sequel."

"Did he want me to call him?" Jeremy rose. "I checked those facts six times each. You know that, Ellie. You helped me." Ellie was his biggest fan and strongest supporter. When he'd sold his first three novels—for a pittance—she'd encouraged him to keep writing, to hone his talent. When he was about to starve to death, she'd bought him lunches and showed up at his door with casseroles. All because she believed in his writing. Now, here he was, in her store, signing his fourth book—and finally gaining national recognition. *Blood on the Moon* was a bestseller. And his editor, Henry Mills, had never had a problem with a single word of it. Jeremy knew the sequel was even better. So what was going on?

"Henry doesn't want you to call. He said he's going to continue working. He also said he wasn't coming to the party tonight." She shrugged her shoulders. "You told me he hated that kind of thing."

"He deserves the party as much as I do," Jeremy pointed out. "He's a great editor."

"Nonetheless, he isn't coming. He said he was so involved in the book he wanted to continue with it.

And—'' she gave him a stern look ''—he told me to tell you to leave the ladies alone.''

"These aren't ladies," Jeremy said, lowering his voice so that only Ellie could hear. "These are fans."

"I've heard about your fan club," Ellie said. "Be careful, Jeremy. There are a lot of desperate women out there, and some of them can read. I've been in the book business a long time, and I've seen it happen more than once. Handsome author stalked by fan. There was even a book about it. I remember something about a mallet."

Jeremy winked at her. "I think I can handle a woman so taken with my writing that she wants me."

"Don't let that Texas-size ego overwhelm that Rhode Island-size brain," Ellie warned him. "Now sign books. The crowd is about to stampede."

Jeremy laughed and turned his attention to the first woman who stood in the queue at his table. As he scanned the crowd, he noticed that about seventy percent were of the female persuasion. And one of them was that very attractive brunette.

She caught his eye again, and he felt his body tingle. Yes indeed, it was going to be nice to ride the wave of stardom that his book had created.

After twenty years of barely being able to afford beans, he was getting the payoff for dedication and hard work. And he intended to enjoy it.

The line moved slowly, and Jeremy talked a moment with each person. His novel about the Texas territory that had once been part of Mexico and a lure for all types of renegades desperate to start a new life had touched his readers in a way he had yet to fully understand. The book had been taken, in part, from some of the stories that had been handed down in his family about his great-grandfather, the legendary Bat Masterson.

To Jeremy, it was a miracle that he'd connected so solidly with his readers. A miracle and one helluva grand experience— He looked up to find the beautiful brunette next in line.

"Mr. Masterson," she said. "I loved your book. My great-great-grandmother was one of the original settlers of Texas. It brought back a lot of the stories my family told. But the book was better—it was almost like living the stories."

"Thank you, Mrs.—" He waited.

"Ms. Gabriel Wexit, fifth-generation Texan."

Jeremy liked the way she laughed. And he liked her brown eyes, and her body. Since his breakup with his last girlfriend, he'd focused completely on his writing—just as he'd vowed to do. But tonight, he had a party to attend and he wanted some female companionship.

"Ms. Wexit, would you like to go to a party tonight?"

"A party?" She gave him a quizzical look.

"At a friend's home. Sort of a celebration for the book. You can meet me there if that's more comfortable for you."

She hesitated half a second. "That sounds lovely."

Jeremy wrote down the time and address on one of his cards and handed it to her. "I'll look forward to seeing you there."

She took the card and let her fingers briefly touch his. "Me, too." Then she took the book he signed for her and left the store.

Jeremy saw Ellie staring at him, and knew he'd earned her disapproval. She was a tyrant when it came to his writing. And though her obsessiveness could be a little irritating, she was the best friend a man could have. He turned his attention back to the line. It was going to be a long afternoon.

The bell jangled as another customer entered. Jeremy didn't bother to look up. He only did so when the woman in front of his table drew in a sharp breath and stepped away from him. The sight that met his eyes made him put down his pen and close the book he had been autographing.

"You sign your name to that book of lies as if you're proud of it," the woman said. She had a long knife hung at her side. He recognized the bone handle design as Apache. It was a ceremonial knife, one used to send an enemy's spirit into the land of his ancestors. His gaze moved from the knife to the rapid movement of her chest as she breathed and a long, dark braid that fell across one shoulder.

"Can I help you, ma'am?" Jeremy asked slowly, staring directly into her angry chocolate-brown eyes. It was a writer's worst nightmare—a fan who was disappointed in a book—and armed. It would require kid gloves to get her placated and out of the store.

"Yes, you can," she said, stepping to the table and leaning down. "Withdraw that book and write history like it really happened." She swept her arm around the room. Everyone who'd been in line backed away from the table. "All of these people believe what you write. They don't understand that fiction is a place where a writer can lie, distort the truth and change history."

Jeremy took another moment to better observe his accuser. She was a beautiful woman, with a willowy grace belying the steel strength he could see beneath her jeans and shirt. Shining black hair, neatly parted, hung in two long braids as thick as ropes. Her complexion was flawless, a burnished tan that spoke of her heritage as well as her love of the outdoors. Had it not been for the fury on her features, she might have been mistaken for a fashion model on a shoot.

"Let me finish this signing, and we can talk about this," he said. The accusation that he'd distorted history stung him more than a little. He'd worked hard, done months of research, to be sure he got his historical facts correct. First Henry, now this woman!

"I have nothing to say to you, except that you're a liar and an impostor. You pretend to write the story of Texas. You pretend to capture the past. What you do is spread old, tired lies about my grandfather." She drew the knife and brought it down in a sharp, clean movement. The blade pierced the wooden table and stuck.

The knife quivered between them, a symbol of her heritage and a statement that she'd come to make a point, not commit an act of violence.

Out of the corner of his eye, he saw Ellie picked up the telephone. He turned his head toward her, meeting her gaze. He knew she was going to call 9-1-1, and he shook his head, signaling Ellie to hold off. If at all possible, he wanted to handle this quietly. He touched the knife handle to show he wasn't afraid. "You're not helping your case, coming here with a weapon," he said.

"If my grandfather was the kind of man you portrayed him as, I wouldn't hesitate to follow in his footsteps and cut out your heart."

The bookstore audience quickly began to move to the exit, but Jeremy didn't care. He stared at the woman who was both a figure of history and incredibly real. He knew instantly who she was talking about. He knew it and he felt a chill. ''Thunder Horse,'' he said softly. He'd never expected to meet a living relative of the great Apache chief.

''My grandfather,'' she answered, standing so straight and tall that he recognized it was pride, not anger, that had driven her to make this public display.

''Is there a problem?'' Ellie took her cue from Jeremy and came out from behind the counter. ''Put the knife away and come in my office. Have a cup of coffee. I'm sure Jeremy can straighten this out when he finishes with the signing. Some of these people have been waiting better than an hour. I know you understand.''

Ellie's cool attempts to move the woman away from Jeremy failed miserably. She held her ground, never even acknowledging Ellie's presence. Her dark eyes held Jeremy's blue ones.

''Tell these people that the man you portray in your book as Thunder Horse is someone you made up. He bears no relationship to the real man, my grandfather.''

Jeremy put his hands on the table and cleared his throat. ''I can't do that, ma'am. I did my research for this book. What I put in it are the facts as recorded in the Texas Historical Archives.'' He felt his own anger begin to build. ''I was very careful. Even though this is a novel, I made sure I had everything right.''

''Lies!'' she cried. ''I am Anna Red Shoes, daughter of Painted Horse, granddaughter of Thunder Horse. My grandfather was not a savage who killed for pleasure. He killed only after he was forced to do so to protect his people.''

Jeremy knew that refuting her version of history would get them nowhere. "I can only offer to talk with you," he said. "I'll be glad to listen to—"

"So that you can steal more stories, and twist and distort them to suit your purposes?" She leaned forward. "There is no talking. I'm camping out with my horses under the sky that was once my grandfather's roof. You have until tomorrow. Either you make a public statement that your portrayal of Thunder Horse is wrong, or—" she was only inches from his face "—I will make sure that you pay the price."

"Young woman," Ellie said in the sharpest tone Jeremy had ever heard her use. "I hope you're not making a threat."

Anna Red Shoes did not seem to be in the least intimidated. She never shifted her gaze from Jeremy as she spoke. "A threat both legal and physical." Her hand clenched only inches above the knife handle. "I make this solemn vow. If you don't correct the lies you've printed, you will suffer. You will suffer greatly, and at my hands."

In a whirl of braids, she was gone.

ANNA FOUND THAT building a fire soothed her nerves. As soon as the flames were leaping in the gathering twilight, she felt her body begin to calm, and then her mind. She'd allowed her emotions to get the better of her. She'd been so angry in the bookstore that she'd lost control. That was unacceptable.

She'd also stormed off and left her knife. She'd called the bookstore, and the woman who answered had frostily told her she'd track it down, and Anna could pick it up in the morning. Well, that was better treatment than she deserved, Anna knew, after her emotional display in the store. But at least she'd get her grandfather's knife back. Unless Jeremy Masterson had it…

She poured a cup of the camp coffee that she loved and settled back against the old cedar stump she'd chosen for that purpose. It was a comfortable place to sit. And the early spring dusk was beautiful.

To the west the sky was a vibrant fuchsia, and from the east where it was already darkening to inky-blue, the first star twinkled down at her. Remembering her father's words, she asked the star to give her light on her journey.

Sighing, she stood up and checked the horses that were hobbled near the campsite. The truth was, she'd need more than guidance. She'd come to the Texas Hill Country in a fit of passion, and she'd let that passion drive her, up until now. She'd confronted Jeremy Masterson, her *former* favorite writer. And what good had it done? None. She didn't feel a bit better, and his wretched book, which painted a vivid picture of her beloved grandfather as a murdering savage, was still selling off the shelves like hotcakes.

Worse than that was the bitter disappointment that was beginning to spoil even the taste of her camp coffee. She returned to the fire and made herself comfortable, allowing the erratic rhythm of the flames to soothe her.

What had she expected? That was the question that she had to ask—and finally answer. Had she really thought that Jeremy Masterson would stand up in public and say, "Oh, my, I may have made a mistake. Maybe my book is wrong"?

She bit her lip and realized that was exactly how

she'd hoped events would turn out. She also knew how silly and naive such an expectation was.

But Jeremy Masterson had been the author she'd loved. His writing about Texas and the vast wilderness that had challenged white and Native American alike, had seduced her. In many ways, he was like a member of her family, but so much more. She'd read all of his books and every one of his stories. She'd hunted down his essays and even the articles he wrote for various Texas newspapers. In his work, he'd shown such a love for the land, for the place called Texas that was as much a part of her as her own skin. And she had fallen in love with him because she felt as if she knew him better than anyone she'd ever known.

And then he'd published *Blood on the Moon.* And shown her that he was like all the others. History didn't matter. Accuracy was out the window. Just throw together a good tale about a savage Indian and a noble white man who saved Texas from a bloodbath, and watch the dollars roll in. Jeremy Masterson had sold out, and even if he never recanted a word, Anna had known that she had to tell him. To his face. In public.

Well, he was told. And now it was time to pack up her horses and go home.

"We'll head back tomorrow," she said aloud, taking comfort in the sound of her own voice and the nearness of the two horses. She'd brought Calamity and Allegro along because she'd intended to spend a few days riding through the Hill Country. Now, though, she only wanted to load up and go back to El Paso where she belonged. It was time for her to get back to her job at the shelter. She groaned as she thought of the probability that someone at the home for abused women would hear of her threatening an author with a knife. In public. It had been a very emotional display, and could carry a hefty price.

Calamity nickered softly, as if to say that going home was a good idea. Anna went to the horse and stroked her neck. It was early April, but the setting sun had taken all of the spring warmth. She'd need her bedroll tonight.

She heated a can of stew on the fire and tossed dry sticks in the low flames. No matter what she did to keep busy, her mind kept going back to Jeremy Masterson. He was more handsome in person than his photo on his book jacket. She could still hear his voice, a real Texas drawl with the prerequisite "ma'am" when he addressed her.

If only he hadn't written those things about her grandfather. Since he was writing fiction, why hadn't he made up a name for the Apache in the book? Everyone else did it. And most didn't bother to do a bit of research about how things really were. No, it was easier to accept the Hollywood version of the past than to struggle with the issues of right and wrong that were on both sides of the Native American question.

In the distance a coyote howled, and Anna listened to the mournful song. Soon there would be so many people living in Texas that there would be no room for the coyote. Like the bear and panther and wolf, he would disappear. Like the red man.

"The past is over and the future can't be counted on," she told herself. She tossed the remains of the coffee in the fire and pulled her blankets over her as she settled on the ground, using her saddle for a pillow.

As a little girl she'd often camped with her grand-

father. He'd survived the trial in which he was accused
of killing a dozen white settlers. He was a very old
man, and Anna had loved to sleep under the stars and
listen to his stories. He'd told her about the wiles of
the coyote and the bravery of the wolf. And the wis-
dom of the buffalo that had once roamed free through
vast stretches of long grass.

Thunder Horse had been over one hundred when he
died on a reservation. But he was not buried there. His
ashes were scattered in the very hills where she now
camped. Tomorrow, before she went home, she would
visit the sacred place where she'd set him free.

The coyote seemed to cry agreement with her plan,
and Anna closed her eyes, determined to sleep. But no
matter how she tried to relax, she could not. She
wasn't satisfied with her meeting with Jeremy Masterson. He hadn't believed her. She'd come all this
way to straighten him out—and all she'd done was
amuse him.

She sat up. She knew where he lived. She'd made
it a point to find out. It wouldn't take long to drive
there. And he had offered to talk with her. Maybe if
she didn't create a public scene, he might actually listen to what she had to say. And she might get her
knife back.

She knew she was fooling herself. There hadn't
been an inch of bend in the man in the bookstore. Not
an inch. But she'd driven a long way, and she wasn't
going home until she tried again.

Throwing off the blankets, she kicked the fire out
and checked the hobbles on the horses. They would
be fine for a while.

"I must be crazy," she said aloud.

Even as she talked, she unhitched the horse trailer,

got in her truck and slowly headed down the rock-strewn path toward the main road. Jeremy lived out near a small community called Hunt. It was only a twenty-minute drive. She could get there, have her say and get back to her horses in an hour.

The clock on the dash showed midnight when she pulled off the main road and down the narrow lane that led to Jeremy's home. The grounds, or what she could see of them in the beams of her truck lights, were well tended. The house, when she finally got to it, was modest and cheerful. There were even flowers blooming in the beds. She wondered if he was a secret gardener or if he paid to have the work done.

As she neared the door, which was well lighted, she noticed an herb patch. She didn't try to stop her smile. This was how she'd imagined Jeremy would live. Bending down, she pinched a few plants and identified basil, lemon dill and mint. She put the herbs in her pocket for luck.

Her knock was bold, and yet it brought no response. She knocked again. The radio was playing inside, and when she waited several minutes and no one came to the door, she moved around to look in an open window. She wasn't a Peeping Tom, but she couldn't resist. It would be a thrill to catch a glimpse of him at work—even if he was no longer her favorite author.

A light burned in what appeared to be a study. A big desk chair faced a computer station against the far wall, where a screen of text glowed brightly. Otherwise, the room looked empty.

As her eyes better adjusted to the dim light of the room, she made out a dark shape on the floor. Even as her eyes registered the outline of a body, her brain tried to resist it. Jeremy Masterson wouldn't sleep on the bare floor. Her impulse was to run—fast. But she couldn't. What if Jeremy was injured? Had suffered a heart attack?

"Hey!" Anna called louder. "Mr. Masterson!" She beat on the window frame, hard.

Jeremy didn't budge.

Anna reached into her pocket, pulled out her pocketknife and cut the screen. The sharp knife zipped through it, and in a matter of seconds there was a hole wide enough for her to slip through.

She jumped to the window ledge and slid through to the floor. Hurrying, she rushed to the body, unaware of the blood until she stepped in it. She knew then she'd made a terrible mistake.

Gently turning the body, she saw first the multiple stab wounds to the chest— Suddenly she realized that the dead man was a stranger. It was not Jeremy Masterson, but someone she'd never seen. There was no help for him. His body was already stiffening with rigor mortis.

The horror of what she saw numbed her. Anna forced herself to remain still, to breathe, to think. Her grandfather had been a man of rigid control. He'd taught her the danger of emotionalism and fear, and Anna reached deep inside herself, seeking that discipline.

Body trembling, she slowly stood and tried to determine what had happened. A stack of manuscript pages sat on the desk, and by them, the computer screen glowed a vivid blue. The full danger and brutality of the scene hit her hard. She couldn't save the dead man, and the worst thing that could happen would be for her to be found with the body.

She ran to the window and climbed back out, then

sprinted across the lawn to her truck. As she drove away and pulled onto the main road, she looked around to make sure no one witnessed her exit from the murder scene.

Chapter Two

In the full light of the Texas moon, the field of blue-bells seemed dusted with silver. Jeremy put his arm around Gabriel. She'd been an enchanting date—she'd read all of his novels and had, twice, actually quoted from *Blood on the Moon*. Jeremy couldn't help but be flattered by such attention from a lovely woman.

"Penny for your thoughts," Gabriel said, as if she knew he was thinking about her.

"It's so beautiful." He pointed out across the meadow. His friends, Mike and Rachel Kettering, had turned an old homestead into a showplace. But then, Texas in the spring was hard to ugly up, he thought with a grin.

"It *is* lovely. And in your books, you describe it just this way. I'll bet you have a million fans writing you." She gave him a teasing look. "And most of them women."

"Hardly that many," Jeremy said, enjoying Gabriel's undivided attention. Earlier, he'd left the book signing, Ellie's demands that he head straight to the Kettering's ranch still ringing in his ears. He'd made one personal detour, and had arrived in plenty of time to help, but as he'd suspected, the hosts had everything under control. He and Mike had spent the time before the party sipping bourbon and swapping yarns. Now he was feeling expansive and relaxed.

"Do you have any really dedicated fans? I've often wondered what it would be like to get mail from absolute strangers."

"Some are stranger than others," Jeremy said, his tone light, but his thoughts heavy. He wouldn't exactly call Anna Red Shoes a fan, but she stayed in his mind. He was glad he'd dissuaded Ellie from reporting the incident to the police. Anna's accusation had stung, and the less attention she got at this point, the better. He preferred to deal with her himself.

He turned his attention to Gabriel's lovely eyes. "*You're* very beautiful. But then, you already know that."

"Want to go for a walk in the moonlight?" she asked, pressing a little closer to him.

Jeremy felt his body's sudden desire to do exactly that. He and Gabriel, alone beneath the moon in a field of bluebells. It was the stuff of fantasies. But he hesitated. His last breakup had been unpleasant, and he'd vowed not to get involved with a woman until he completed the sequel to his novel. In his opinion, women and writing didn't mix well. Both of them were jealous mistresses.

"I was actually thinking of going home," he said.

"It's only midnight," Gabrielle whispered. "Come on, Jeremy." Her voice was almost a purr. "Let's have a little privacy."

He briefly tightened his hold on her shoulders. "Ah, you're a tempting woman," he said. He bent to brush his lips across her neck. "But I've taken a vow to finish my next book before I allow myself the luxury of a woman's company.''

She laughed. "A vow. How monastic! Do you write in a robe?"

He joined in her laughter. "You have a definite way of painting a picture," he said. "Maybe you should write."

She turned away from him. "There are too many writers in Texas already. By the way, I was sort of expecting Blane Griffin to be here. I read somewhere that you two were best friends."

Jeremy tried not to react. His friendship with Blane was over, and all because of a woman. It was one more reminder not to allow the very tempting Gabriel to lead him off the path toward his next novel. Besides, he needed to talk with Henry.

"Blane and I grew up together," he said. "And I do have to go home. My editor isn't happy with my latest book. We need to have a conversation."

"At midnight? What am I, a pumpkin?"

There was frustration in her voice, and he put his hands on her shoulders and held her gently. "I'd like to get to know you better, Gabriel, but I've worked for twenty years for this opportunity. I can't afford to mess it up because I meet a woman who makes writing a second choice."

She turned in his arms. "Do I do that?"

"I'm afraid you could," he said, brushing a strand of her dark hair from her face. "I'm known to be a man who likes a gamble, but I'm walking away from this one. I'd like to call you, later, when I'm free to…pursue this." •

She stared into his eyes. "That's your decision." Her lips curved into a forced smile. "Not mine. I don't put my life on hold for any man. Not even Jeremy Masterson, famous author.''

"You are a spunky little thing," he said, leading her toward the doorway and the party that was in full swing. "I'll call you when I come up for air. I promise."

Jeremy never saw the hand that came out of nowhere and slapped Gabriel across the face. He did, however, recognize the sultry voice of Lucinda Estar.

"You conniving little witch." Lucinda made a grab for Gabriel's hair, but Jeremy caught her wrist. It had been a long, emotional day, and Lucinda was the finishing touch.

"Lucinda, you're drunk," he said in a monotone. "Straighten up before you humiliate yourself."

"I don't have to work at *that*. You've done a thorough job of it. Every time I turn my back, you're with some cheap little tramp," she said, her voice slurring a little. She was unsteady on her feet, and Jeremy found himself in the uncomfortable position of supporting her so she didn't fall.

Gabriel gave him a long, pitying look. "I didn't realize you had a full plate." She walked away without looking back.

"You told me you had to finish your book," Lucinda said, her voice growing louder. "What was *she*? Research? You dumped me for her?"

The entire party had ground to a halt, and everyone was staring at him and the drunken woman he held up. Jeremy searched the room with his eyes until he finally saw Ellie. She hurried to his side, her face clearly showing her concern. "Please call Blane," Jeremy said.

"Are you sure that's a good idea?" Ellie asked.

"No choice. He needs to collect Lucinda before she does more damage to herself."

"Or you," Ellie said archly. "Your personal life is going to catch up with you, Jeremy."

"I don't need a lecture, I need some help." Jeremy didn't mean to snap but his patience was gone. He slid Lucinda onto a sofa.

"Do you really think Blane wants her back? Again?"

Jeremy heard the hardness in Ellie's tone. She'd never said anything about his rash affair with Lucinda. She didn't have to. Everyone in Texas knew it had ruined his lifelong friendship with Blane Griffin.

"Just call him. He can make up his mind if he wants her or not."

"And you?" Ellie asked.

"I'm going home."

Jeremy didn't have a chance to take more than one step before he felt the hand on his shoulder. "Running away again?"

He turned toward the angry face of Blane Griffin. "I'm not running, I'm withdrawing. Let's don't do this, Blane. Lucinda's drunk, and you and I have both had more than a couple. This isn't the time to try to settle our differences."

"I turn my back, and she's over here, tracking after you like a dog in—" He broke off and turned away.

Jeremy looked around the room at his friends who'd come to celebrate the success of his book. He and Blane had started out in the writing business together. His career had taken a sudden swing up, but Blane was still toiling in the trenches. "Can I get a couple of drinks here?" he said to one of his friends.

In a moment he had two bourbons in his hand. He

offered one to Blane. "Let's have a toast. To the future. I'm sure your bestseller is just around the corner."

His old friend's gaze held his for a moment. "You're one helluva hypocrite," Blane said, putting the drink down without tasting it. He grabbed Lucinda's arm, hauled her off the sofa and stalked toward the door. Then he turned back abruptly, his lean face hard. "My star is rising, Jeremy. It's you who needs a toast, not me. I've just spoken with your editor, and he's buying my book. He thinks it's better than your sequel. So when you decide to pour liquor and offer up a toast of hope, maybe you should drink it to yourself."

With Lucinda firmly in his grasp, Blane walked out.

Jeremy felt like a fool. He'd intended to mend fences with Blane, but what he'd done was widen the breach. The toast had probably been an idiotic idea, but it had been sincere.

A hush had fallen over the party. He turned to see Ellie staring at the doorway through which Blane had just departed. Picking up one of the drinks, he said, "To cowboys, literature and a bit of moon madness. We all suffer from it now and again." He downed the bourbon and was relieved to see the tension break and the party pick up again.

"What book did Blane sell Henry?" Ellie asked, suddenly appearing at his shoulder.

"I'm not certain. Henry said something about something set around—"

"The Alamo?"

Jeremy arched his eyebrows. "That was it."

"Back when Blane was in a slump over Lucinda, I

talked with him some about his book.'' Ellie laughed. ''Who would have thought Henry would buy it?''

''I'm glad for him,'' Jeremy said. ''Though I wish he'd been a little more gracious.''

''And shown better taste in women,'' Ellie added. ''Let's have another drink.''

IT WAS AFTER MIDNIGHT when Jeremy finally turned down the long, secluded drive to his house. He felt a little guilty about having left Henry alone all evening—but only a little. Henry had obviously been a very busy man. Not only had he bought Blane's book, but he'd talked to Ellie about how the editing was going. Sure, Ellie was his best friend, but Jeremy's writing was a very personal thing. On top of that, Henry had chosen not to attend the party. Well, it was *his* loss.

The house was dark, and Jeremy entered as quietly as he could. He was glad that Henry had decided to go to bed. He didn't want to talk about work—his or Blane's.

Easing down the darkened hallway toward his bedroom, Jeremy caught the glow of the computer screen reflecting off the panes of the window. He stopped. Henry was like an old maid about some things—especially computers. He'd never go to bed with text on the screen.

Jeremy entered his study and stopped, stunned, as he saw the outline of the body on the floor. He moved forward automatically, then knelt beside the body.

''Henry.'' He shook him gently. It wasn't until Henry didn't respond that he allowed the terrible thought to come. ''Oh, no.'' He rolled the body over and saw the dark blood, the stab wounds. ''My God.''

It came out as a croak through the knot of horror in his throat. "What in the hell happened here?"

He crossed the room and snapped on the overhead light. The scene was out of a nightmare. Blood had pooled beside the editor. Two sets of bloody tracks were distinct—his own, and another pair leading toward the window.

Jeremy forced his body not to move. He carefully took in the scene. The desk was a jumble, as if a struggle had taken place. From the position of the body, the bloody tracks, the open window where the cut screen flapped in the night breeze, it seemed clear that someone had come in through the window.

Henry Mills had been murdered. Someone had slipped into the house and killed him. But why? It didn't take a rocket scientist to figure out that whomever had done it very likely had killed the wrong man. Jeremy was certain that he had been the intended target.

"Henry," he said softly. The reality of his editor's death was like a kick in the gut. Henry had been a kind man. And now he was dead because he had been in the wrong place at the wrong time.

Jeremy's first impulse was to call the sheriff. He even reached for the phone. But his fingers never picked up the receiver. He turned instead to study the tracks. He didn't write about the West for nothing. He was a skilled rancher, and a man who'd grown up in the outdoors. He could read a set of tracks as well as—or better than—most. He studied the small footprints and determined they belonged to a small man or a woman. His best guess was a woman. The foot was slender, delicate, and wearing western boots.

The scene in the bookstore came back to him. *Anna*

Red Shoes. She'd had on jeans and boots. And she'd vowed to make him suffer. She'd threatened to harm him—legally and physically. Those were her words. And a knife had been her chosen weapon.

He stood up and looked around the room. He almost didn't see the knife. It had been dropped at the window and had fallen behind the draperies. Even before he walked over to more closely examine it, he recognized the bone-carved handle as a ceremonial blade used by Apache Indians. He'd done enough research to recognize the knife, which was used specifically for ceremonial kills.

He'd also seen a similar knife very recently. In the hand of Anna Red Shoes. Her name was all but written in Henry's blood. He knelt and felt the bloody tracks in the carpet. He wasn't that far behind her, and there was no time to waste. He went to his closet and pulled out his hunting gear, including his Marlin 30-30. The problem with calling the sheriff was that Lem Polluck was sheriff in name only. He was a popular man who meant well, but he wasn't a tracker or a hunter. And he didn't have a brilliant record of crime solving.

Lem was no match for a cold-blooded killer who was the granddaughter of Thunder Horse. He'd only muddy up the trail, confuse things.

Jeremy made a quick decision. He'd track Anna and as soon as he captured her, he'd call the sheriff to make the arrest.

Jeremy checked the gun, grabbed ammunition and went to his truck. One good thing about research was that he knew enough about the history of Anna's forebearers to start his search for her. He'd bet dollars to doughnuts that he knew exactly where she was. There was a place on the west side of town that had been sacred to Thunder Horse. And Anna had mentioned something about camping. That was the place to hunt for her.

He made sure his cell phone was in his pack so he could call Lem as soon as he found her.

ANNA SHIFTED TO HER left side on the hard earth. Not thirty feet away, Calamity and Allegro grazed peacefully. The sound of the horses' strong teeth pulling at the rough grass was soothing. When dawn broke, she'd saddle up and ride to the place where she'd scattered her grandfather's ashes, the place that had once been sacred to her people—before it was stolen from them. Once she paid her respects, she'd pack up and head for home. The entire trip had been a fool's errand.

She drifted into a light sleep, deviled by nightmares of bodies, and a tall, broad-shouldered man who taunted her. He held a book and seemed to be laughing at her.

Anna wasn't certain exactly what brought her to full wakefulness, but she opened her eyes and saw that her fire was still high. She realized that the horses had stopped grazing. One of them blew out a loud snort.

Anna listened.

The sound of a truck engine suddenly stopped. Instead of sitting up, she forced herself to remain perfectly still in her bedroll, but her fingers found the small knife that she always kept beside her. Her rifle was only a foot away. She wasn't a hunter—had never killed for food or fear. But she knew how to do it.

But this wasn't a coyote or panther searching for dinner. This was a creature far more deadly.

Whomever it was came up the hillside with great

care. Only the slip of a piece of shale, the rustle of winter grass not yet green and springy, gave away the progress of the stalker. Anna's grip tightened on the knife, and she kept her breathing regular and easy as she waited.

She rethought her steps. The hillside she'd chosen for her campsite was a place where her people had once camped. Below her the Guadeloupe River gurgled over flat, smooth rocks. To her knowledge, the land was not used by anyone, so she hadn't bothered to seek permission. The person creeping up to her campsite might only be the landowner checking to see who was on his property. If that was the case, she didn't want to act rashly. After all, she was the trespasser. Under the circumstances it would be better to remain calm and then explain her reasons for being there.

But as she listened to the stranger's approach, she knew better. The person headed her way was sneaking, taking great care to hide his arrival. That meant that he hoped to surprise her—and that, in turn, meant only one thing. Trouble.

She didn't move, though she could feel her heart thumping hard in her chest.

She heard him, now only ten yards away as he came up on the level with the campsite. Though her back was to him, she could feel him staring at her. She imagined what he saw: a lone camper turned on her side, face to the cheerful fire.

One of the horses stomped the ground and blew hard, a wheezing sound that spoke of distrust and fear. She wanted to speak to the horse, to calm her, but she kept silent. She wanted the stalker to get closer—close enough that she could jump him.

She felt his approach. He made no sound, but she didn't need her ears to tell her what was happening. Every one of her senses was attuned. She held the knife tightly, ready for her chance. It was as if her grandfather were beside her, whispering into her ear, telling her to be calm, to be brave, to wait for the exact moment.

That moment arrived.

Anna whipped out of the blankets, rolling low and fast and with enough momentum that when she caught the stalker in his lower legs with the full thrust of her body, she knocked him off balance. Before he could recover, she was on her feet and in a headlong tackle.

She brought him down with a satisfactory *thud*. To make certain that his lungs were empty, she threw herself across him and allowed her full body weight to land on his chest and ribs. She heard a *whoosh* of air, then rolled off him, stood and brought her boot-clad foot squarely into his chest area, connecting soundly with his sternum.

"Auuugh!"

It was the sound she wanted to hear. She pressed the point of her knife into his throat. "I don't know who you are, but you're one breath away from dying," she said as she allowed the blade to prick the skin.

Chapter Three

"Who are you and what do you want?"

Jeremy didn't try to answer. He was too busy trying to breathe. But he wasn't too badly winded to understand that he'd made a serious miscalculation. One that could have an expensive price tag. He felt the trickle of blood on his neck where the point of Anna's knife barely broke his skin.

"You're in enough trouble," he said. "Don't make it worse." Of course, that was ridiculous. She'd already killed one man. They couldn't hang her twice.

There was a sudden intake of breath, and Jeremy knew that she'd recognized him. His body tensed, but he didn't move. To do so would have invited bloodshed. His own.

"I knew you were a liar when I read your book," Anna said, her voice low and deadly. "I didn't know you were a coward. What did you intend to do, sneak up here and bushwhack me?"

Jeremy pondered her question. She was darn good at turning a situation to her advantage. It was almost as if she weren't aware of her own actions. He had read enough psychology to know that a sociopath never had regret for anything she did. Anna Red Shoes was displaying classic symptoms.

"We can work this out," he said calmly. "There's no reason for anyone else to get hurt."

"Anyone else?"

He had to give it to her. She was smart. And alert. And she could playact with the best of them. Or else she was crazier than he'd thought—a scary possibility—because she sounded completely innocent.

"What happened to Henry was a mistake, okay?" He felt a twinge of betrayal of his friend. What had happened wasn't a mistake—it was cold-blooded. But he had to talk himself out of a tight situation. And if Anna was as crazy as she acted, then maybe—

"What happened to Henry—and who is he?"

"My editor." He took a breath, glad at last that his lungs were working normally. "He was stabbed to death."

He'd expected some reaction, but he got nothing. In the darkness he couldn't see her features, but he could feel her slender body tense beside him as she kept the pressure on the knife steady. Not even a flinch.

"You think I killed him?" Her voice was cold, emotionless.

"I don't think you meant to kill Henry. You intended to kill me."

He expected the blade of the knife to punish him for those words. Anna never even breathed.

When she did speak, it wasn't what he'd expected to hear. "The most interesting thing about all of this is your arrogance."

Jeremy was shocked at the matter-of-fact tone. "My arrogance? What are you talking about?"

"Your editor is killed in your home, and *your* biggest concern is that someone meant to kill you."

If Jeremy had had any doubts about Anna's guilt, they evaporated. She'd given herself away. He'd never said anything about the murder being at his home. And the only two people who knew about the murder were him, *and the murderer.*

He felt the tip of the knife shift.

"What's wrong? Cat got your tongue?" she asked. "Or did I hit a little too close to home?"

He had to be careful. She was very angry, and he couldn't patronize her or ignore her. He had to talk with her as if she were rational. "I came out here to bring you in. I didn't want to leave it to chance, or to someone else. I wanted to make sure that Henry's murderer was apprehended and brought to justice."

"You're not only arrogant, you're completely blind. You're so totally self-absorbed that you don't even see the truth of your actions."

The knife blade moved away, and for one second Jeremy considered attacking her. But before he could put impulse to action, he felt the blow across his temple. He didn't pass out, but he was stunned. When he felt the bite of the rope around his wrists and ordered his body to fight, his arms and legs refused to obey. Then it was too late. He was trussed like Tom Turkey at Thanksgiving.

ANNA TIED THE LAST knot and snugged the rope tight. It would be several hours before Jeremy Masterson wiggled his way out of the mess he was in. By then, she'd be long gone.

"You better give yourself up," Jeremy said as she stood.

He was coming back to his senses, what few he had. "Take some free advice," she said. "Don't give guidance to the person you came to apprehend when you're the one tied up like a big ol' hog."

Her words angered him, and it made her happy.

"You're not just walking out of here."

There was a challenge in his tone, and she had to admire his spirit. He was tied, and she could easily injure him, but he didn't back down.

"No, I'm going to drive out of here. Today's Friday. I'll give the authorities a call Sunday morning and make sure you got loose." The idea of leaving him on the cold, hard ground for a long stretch of time was immensely gratifying. For a man with Jeremy Masterson's machismo and ego, each minute would be a grueling and humiliating eternity.

"Better check out your rig. I don't think you're going anywhere."

His tone held just enough smugness to alert Anna. She made sure the horses were fine and then went to her truck and trailer. The light from the moon was enough to reveal the flat tires: four of them—two on the truck and two on the horse trailer. And they had been cut to the point that they couldn't be repaired.

"You lowlife son of a—" She broke off. She wouldn't give him the pleasure of letting him know he'd gotten to her. But how in the hell was she going to get home with four flats? As he no doubt had guessed, she had a spare for the truck and one for the trailer. That still left her two short.

"What's the trouble?" he called out. "You got a flat?"

Anna walked back to him. In the moonlight she could make out only the rough edges of his features.

He was a big man with a prominent jaw and dark hair. "If I were a killer, I'd finish you right now," she said. "Think about that tomorrow when the sun comes up and you get thirsty."

She picked up the saddle and went to work on Calamity.

"You're a fool if you think you can ride out of the state of Texas on horseback. I'll have the law after you so fast—"

"I grew up in these foothills with my father, who grew up with Thunder Horse. We know this land. If I choose to disappear into the hills, you'll never find me."

"That sounds like the boast of an inexperienced woman."

Anna tightened the girth on Calamity. Then she took out a kerchief and went to Jeremy.

"This is going to give me as much pleasure as it bothers you." She tied the gag tightly, but not so tightly that it might choke him.

He struggled against her, making a sound of protest.

"Along with your immediate dilemma, perhaps you should ponder your chauvinism, bigotry and laziness." She rolled up her bedroll. "I believe people can change. I believe they can see the error of their ways and honestly desire to live a better life. But I think such a conversion comes only after much suffering." She gathered up the lead rope for Allegro and swung into the saddle. "If you like, you can look at me as your spiritual guide. I've put you in a position where you can ponder your shortcomings and grow into a better human being."

She touched her heels to her horse's side, and Calamity spurted forward, Allegro right behind her.

Anna heard Jeremy yell something at her, but she didn't try to understand the garbled threat.

For all of her bravado, she knew she was in serious trouble. Jeremy had come after her for the murder of the man at the computer. She'd pretended to be ignorant of the killing, but she wasn't. She was innocent, but not ignorant. And eventually, if anyone asked the right questions, she'd have to answer with the truth.

The problem was that she knew the workings of the law. She had publicly threatened Jeremy. Once they placed her at the scene of the crime with motive and opportunity, they wouldn't look any farther for the real killer. She would be a convenient suspect; the case would be closed. Chances were good that she'd be convicted. Jeremy Masterson was an influential man, and it was clear that he was determined to blame the murder on her. She'd publicly embarrassed him, and now she was going to pay.

Her only hope was to put as much distance as possible between herself and the writer. With a little luck, she'd be deep into the wild country before he got out of the knots she'd tied. Her ace in the hole was her friends. She knew people all over the area. And they'd help her. If she could just get to Maria Gonzalez, she knew her childhood friend would loan her a vehicle and help her cross the border to Mexico, just until things calmed down.

The idea of running irked Anna, but she was a realist. After a week or so, if he didn't catch Anna first, the sheriff would be forced to look for another suspect in the murder.

Perhaps even Jeremy.

Anna played out a series of possibilities. Perhaps Jeremy's editor hadn't liked the new book. Perhaps they'd had a fight and the editor had refused the book. Jeremy's ego was so big, he might have lost his temper and killed his editor.

It was possible, wasn't it?

JEREMY STRUGGLED until he felt the ropes rub his wrists raw. Anna had ridden off and left him with his feet pulled behind him and tied to his hands and neck. Every time he tried to free himself, the ropes pulled tighter. It was a classic hog-tie—something Anna must have been taught by an old cowboy or a rodeo rider. Or perhaps her grandfather.

Well, it might take him a little while to get free, but when he did… He twisted his hands and, losing patience, pulled at the ropes. His only reward was that the loop around his neck tightened a little more. Now the rope was a constant pressure. He was furious. He knew that if he didn't get free, someone would eventually find him—and the humiliation would be worse than dying.

As he tried to calm down and work the ropes, he focused his mind on images of what he would do to Anna when he caught her. That he'd underestimated her was obvious. He'd sneaked up on her as if she were an average female. For all his research and all his savvy, he'd failed to consider that Anna Red Shoes might be as good in the wilderness as he was.

He felt the rope on his left wrist loosen slightly and he concentrated on getting his hand through. But despite the millimeters of progress he made, he couldn't get free of the ropes. This was going to take a long, long time.

Three hours later he finally shucked the bonds off his hands. In a matter of moments his feet were free and he rolled and stood. When the circulation began to come back to his feet and hands, he felt as if he'd just escaped a bed of fire ants.

Hopping and cursing, he headed for his truck. He didn't even bother to utter an oath when he saw the four flat tires. Anna had done him one better.

But he had a secret weapon.

Unless she'd taken it.

He went to the pack he'd stowed in the truck and opened it. Everything was there, including the cell phone. He dialed the number he knew by heart.

"Ellie?"

"Do you know what time it is?" Ellie asked, more amazed than upset.

"I need your help."

He could tell that his words and tone had awakened her completely.

"What is it?"

"I'm sorry, this is going to be a shock. Henry's been murdered—in my house. I'm after the killer. Remember that woman who came to the signing?"

"Oh, my Lord," Ellie said, coming fully awake. "She threatened to make you pay for what you've written."

"That's her."

"Why would she kill Henry?" Ellie's voice contained the shock and grief that Jeremy hadn't allowed himself to feel. Tender emotions were for women. Anger was what he wanted to feel. And he wanted it now more than ever.

"It looks like she sneaked into the house and stabbed him. There was some kind of struggle. I can only guess that she thought he was me, and that once she started she couldn't stop herself."

"Was there evidence it was her?"

"A knife. Just like the one she left in the bookstore. I found it in the room. It's still there."

"What did the sheriff say?" Ellie asked.

"I haven't called Lem. I'm on the woman's trail. I want to bring her in myself."

"Jeremy, this isn't one of your books. This is real life. Oh, my heavens, I can't believe Henry is dead."

"Ellie, the important thing is catching this woman and making her pay. I almost had her…" He hesitated and decided against giving any more detail. It would only shake Ellie's confidence if she knew he'd been hornswoggled by Anna Red Shoes. And it wouldn't do much for his reputation, either.

"I need a couple of horses," he continued. "A good riding horse and something to pack some supplies on. I need a week's worth of food."

"Jeremy, I'll get you the horses and supplies." She took a deep breath. "What about Henry's body?"

"Give me a few hours' lead. Then call Lem."

"Where are you, and why don't you take some of your own horses?"

There was no way around the truth here, but Jeremy knew he'd tell only as much as he had to. He gave her directions first. "I'm stranded. She slashed my tires."

"You already went after her alone—and she got away?"

He could hear Ellie's panic building. "This is between me and her."

"Even you're not macho enough to believe this makes anything up to Henry, are you? Henry's dead."

Jeremy scowled, though he didn't try to deny the truth of her words. He heard the echo of Anna Red

Shoes's comments and it only made him madder. At this point he was after one thing—revenge.

"I have to do this," he said.

"You don't have to. You *want* to."

He took a breath. Arguing was senseless. "Are you going to help me?"

"Do I have a choice?"

"No. I'm going after her, one way or another."

"I'll bring the horses. But when I get home I'm calling Lem. You can have that much of a headstart on the law."

It was all he was going to get, and Jeremy knew it. Once Ellie made up her mind, there was no changing it. "Bring me some fast horses, then."

"I'll be there in an hour."

WHEN THE FIRST LICK of pink brightened the horizon, Anna pushed Calamity into a trot. She'd walked during the night, afraid of the potholes and stumps that could easily cripple a horse and kill a rider. But with day breaking, she picked a level pass between the hills and began to cover some ground.

She had no doubt that as soon as Jeremy Masterson untied himself, he'd be after her. As soon as he found a way home. She grinned. Instead of damaging his tires, she'd only let the air out, but she'd made sure there wasn't a compression tank in his truck. He'd have a long walk back to civilization.

Anna had never met Henry Mills, but she regretted his death. He'd been stabbed several times, as if he'd tried to defend himself. The more she thought about it, the more it seemed the finger of guilt pointed at Jeremy. Who else in the area would have any bone to pick with an editor from New York?

Unless, of course, Henry's death was an accident and Jeremy *had* been the intended target.

In that case, the list of suspects was endless. Jeremy was a ladies' man and that was a quick ticket to trouble. No telling how many women were angry with him and eager for his hide.

A woman would need the advantage of surprise. It wasn't an easy thing to kill someone. She'd heard her grandfather speak of such things and knew that he told the truth.

Anna found that she was blinking back tears, and they weren't from the bright sun that now struck her full in the face. She was mad at herself when she realized they were from self-pity. She now found herself in a situation where there were no good choices.

She was running from Jeremy Masterson, and soon the law would be behind him. She was accused of a crime she hadn't committed, but if they captured her, she felt certain no one would believe her. And why? Because of who she was.

The situation mirrored the same predicament in which her grandfather had found himself in. Accused of a series of brutal murders that he hadn't committed, he'd also run—deep into the wilderness, into the land that was supposed to belong to him and his people. He'd tried to develop a life as far away from the white settlers as possible.

But every murder that took place on the Texas range had been blamed on him.

The history books had convicted him without benefit of a trial or even of reading his version of the truth.

Anna's hand drifted to Calamity's saddlebag. The handwritten document she'd labored over was still there, still safe. But she'd been a total fool to think that Jeremy Masterson might look at it.

Like all the others, he didn't care about truth. He only wanted a good story. And a scapegoat.

Chapter Four

Jeremy shaded his eyes against the glare of the sun as he studied the tracks. For the past two hours, he'd been following Anna's trail. She'd allowed her horse only a walk during the night, as any horseman would have done. Now the tracks showed she'd picked up her pace: she was trotting. He guessed that this was the point when daybreak had given her the advantage of sight.

His watch showed nine o'clock. By his calculation, she was three hours ahead of him. That wasn't bad, considering that she'd had a good six-hour start. He was steadily gaining on her. With a little luck, he'd have her before the close of day. And this time he wouldn't be foolish enough to underestimate her.

He urged his horse forward into a steady lope. The footing was good, and he intended to make the most of it. Ellie had provided him with two of her best horses. Things were definitely in his favor.

He heard the *chirp* of the cell phone in his pack and stopped to answer it.

"Lem and the deputies are at the campsite," Ellie said without preamble. "He's mad as a hornet and threatening to put *me* in jail. Once he saw all the flats, it wasn't hard for him to figure that someone brought you horses.''

"If Lem tries to blame you, I'll straighten him out. You won't do more than a day or two of jail time."

"This is no time to be flip." Ellie's voice rose in anger. "I overheard some of the men talking, Jeremy, and they weren't shy about saying that maybe you killed Henry."

"Me?" Jeremy couldn't hide his astonishment. "Me?"

"The man is dead in your home, and you're out chasing a woman. They're saying this Anna Red Shoes may be your accomplice. They're implying that the scene in the bookstore was staged. By you. A publicity stunt."

"You've got to be kidding."

"I wish I were." Ellie sighed. "Lem is very angry, and there's more bad news."

Jeremy waited.

"Blane Griffin's heading the tracking team."

"Oh, for pity's sake." Jeremy wanted to crush the small telephone. "Has he called a press conference yet?" It would be just like Blane to try to capitalize on the horrible murder.

"You guessed it. The television crews are arriving right now. They're doing a live feed at the campsite. And they're listing you as a wanted suspect."

"Well—" There wasn't anything Jeremy could say that wouldn't offend Ellie. "Lem isn't buying into this, is he?"

"I can't tell for certain," Ellie admitted. "He's mad about the way you handled it. Blane has been gnawing on his ear all morning. They've even got a national news crew coming in. It seems that the popularity of your novel, the fact that Henry was your editor—all of that is national news. Even the tabloid shows are scheduled to come in. Blane had the nerve to ask if I would host a show in the bookstore.''

Jeremy wanted to bite nails—and then spit them into the lid of Blane's coffin.

"The sensible thing to do is come home and handle all of this mess," Ellie said.

"No."

"Jeremy, you pigheaded son of a gun, you're only making matters worse. You'd better get back home and take care of this."

"No."

"At least talk to Lem."

Jeremy hesitated. He needed to talk with the sheriff, if only to protest his innocence. But talking would do no good. Lem would order him to come back, and when he didn't he would be in a worse situation than he was now.

"I can't do it, Ellie. I have to finish this. I'm gaining on her. I'll have her by nightfall. I'm sure of it."

"When Lem asks me for the number to your cell phone, I'm going to give it to him, and you'd better have a pretty speech thought up. I've seen you charm the pants off ladies and convince the moon to shine just for you. This time, Jeremy, you'd better be at the top of your form—you're in serious trouble."

"I'll be back with her before tomorrow morning." He punched the Off button and put the phone in his pack. Now it couldn't ring. It was the only way he had of making sure he didn't talk to Lem.

"Come on, Jetta," he said to the mare as he pressed his legs on her. "We've got a lot of ground to cover."

Though the tracking absorbed him, Jeremy still had

time to worry. He conceded that perhaps he was guilty of rushing off half-cocked in his pursuit of Anna. But never in his wildest dreams had he thought that he might be considered a suspect in the killing of his editor. It was one of the most absurd things he'd ever heard.

Aside from the fact that he wasn't psychologically capable of murdering anyone, the physical evidence was against such a possibility. What about the small footprints? He wanted to call Lem up and ask the sheriff about that. What did they think? That he'd bought a pair of lady's boots and painstakingly made the prints just to leave a false trail? It was ridiculous! His anger skyrocketed.

This was all Blane's doing. Jeremy had to hand it to the man. Blane had seen a perfect opportunity to even the score, and he'd taken it. Now he would receive the national attention that he so desperately wanted. At Jeremy's expense.

This was all a media game to Blane, and Lem was so simpleminded that he didn't realize it. Ellie had said one theory was that Anna Red Shoes was his accomplice. What straight-thinking person could ever believe that? Why would he need an accomplice? And why her? It didn't make a lick of sense.

Well, when he caught her and brought her in, he'd straighten it all out. And there would be hell to pay. If Blane thought he could turn Henry's death to his advantage, he had had another think coming. He was going to burn him bad.

Jeremy came to a small creek and let the horses drink. He'd cross the Guadeloupe River in a few hours. By then it would be very hot and he'd be ready for a quick dip in the April-cold water. The horses would need a little break, too. They'd been pushing steadily.

He checked his watch and urged his horses forward. He was pushing them hard, he knew, but if he played his cards right, he'd have the woman he pursued, and then Ellie's horses could be returned to the pasture for a good rest.

For the moment, though, he had to ride hard, fast and with extreme caution. He couldn't afford to approach Anna Red Shoes with less than total concentration.

ANNA STOPPED at the river and unsaddled Calamity. It was time to change horses, but she also needed a break. It was well after noon and she hadn't eaten all day. The horses, too, needed some grass.

By her calculation she was at least eight hours ahead of Jeremy. No matter how good a tracker Jeremy hired, they couldn't travel any faster than she was going. In places the terrain was too rugged. The ground was dry and hard, and on the steep inclines, the shale broke loose under the weight of her horse. That made going slow. But it would be as slow for her pursuers as it was for her.

She had time for a little bite to eat and, maybe, to stick her toes in the river. The Guadeloupe was a beautiful crystal-green, and though she knew the water would be cold, it was also inviting.

Once she removed the saddle and packs, the horses rolled in the grass that was just turning green. For all of the trouble she was in, the sight gave her a rush of pleasure.

The land around her was not familiar, but Anna didn't doubt her ability to find her way to Maria Gonzalez's spread. It was due west. To confuse the posse that she knew would be after her, she'd zigged and zagged a bit, but she was still on course.

She gave the horses a meager ration of the grain she'd brought and took out a peanut butter sandwich for herself. She wanted a cup of coffee, but she had no intention of taking the time to build a fire. Later, when she camped for the night, she'd indulge in something hot.

Sitting on a flat rock in the sun, munching her sandwich, Anna had a twinge of conscience. Jeremy Masterson had gotten what he deserved, but it bothered her just a little. She wasn't in the habit of tying men up and abandoning them.

She hadn't had any choice. Still, it worried her. It was early spring and therefore unlikely that snakes would be out—but anything could happen. She shook her head. Jeremy was too tough to attract a predator. Not even a bear could stomach that man!

Still… She stood up, unable to relax. Ultimately she'd have to answer for her actions. And for the accusations that had been hurled unjustly at her. When she did, she wanted a good lawyer at her side. History was not going to repeat itself.

She forced herself to sit down and lean against her saddle. The sun was warm. She was content with the food she'd eaten. She closed her eyes and tried to summon the serenity to rest for a few moments. The horses needed a break, and it behooved her to try and grab twenty minutes, too. Then she could wash her face and get back on the trail.

Anna heard the call of a red-winged blackbird, and that was the last thing she remembered until she opened her eyes. She could tell by the sun that at least two hours had passed. Her first impulse was to panic, but then she realized she was still far ahead of the men who would be tracking her.

Calamity and Allegro were grazing peacefully only ten yards away. Everything was fine.

She walked down to the river and took off her boots and then her pants. Sticking her toes in, she realized the water was even colder than she'd assumed. Too cold for a swim, but perfect to wash the sleepiness away. She knelt down, cupped her hands and brought the water to her face.

She was beside a clear pool where the current gurgled and sang, and she listened to the tune of the river. Her grandfather had once told her a story about a young maiden who'd looked into the water and seen her lover's face. It was a romantic but lovely story… Anna bent lower, staring into the crystal water.

She was completely unprepared when her feet slipped on the rock. Before she could catch herself, she tumbled into the icy water. The shock was so intense that when she came up for air, she was gasping.

Anna felt as if she'd been shot. Her flannel shirt, sopping, tugged her beneath the surface. She worked the buttons and slipped out of it, flopping it up on the rock.

The current was stronger than it had first seemed, and Anna clutched at the rock until she regained her wind and her composure. The moment struck her as funny, and she chuckled at the stupidity of her situation.

Now that she was over the initial shock of the water, she found that it wasn't as cold as she'd first assumed. In fact, it was downright pleasant, even if the current was a little fast for her taste. She let go of the rock, swam to the center of the deep pool and began to swim against the current. After the long hours in the saddle, the free sensation of swimming was wonderful.

Realizing that she hadn't packed additional clothes, Anna took off her under-things and threw them up on the bank in the sun. She wanted to dry them before she rode on. Naked, she gave herself to the cold water and the hot sun and memories of a childhood of freedom.

FOAM LATHERED Jetta's neck as Jeremy pushed the mare harder. He was closing in on Anna. He could tell. On the top of a rise he pulled to a halt and scanned the small valley below him.

The Guadeloupe shimmered through a break of cottonwood trees. On his first examination, Jeremy spotted the Appaloosa grazing on the bank of the river. He had found Anna Red Shoes!

"Easy, Jetta," he said to the mare as he backed her away. The horse he was leading had pricked up her ears and was getting ready to call out to the horses by the river.

"Shush!" he ordered, turning his mount away and heading both horses back down the hill. When he came to a grove of cedars, he got off and tied them up. The rest of the journey he'd make on foot.

He pulled the Marlin 30-30 out of his sheath, and checked it and his pistol to be sure they were loaded. Even as he did it, he felt melodramatic. Anna Red Shoes might be the granddaughter of a famous Native warrior and a murderer, but she was just a woman.

One that had bested him already, he reminded himself. She wasn't someone to play around with. He hefted the rifle and a pair of binoculars, and started back up to the hillside.

He traveled north along the crest of the hill until he found several large rocks and some scrub cedars that made a good hiding place. He wedged himself among the boulders and pulled out the binoculars.

His gaze swept over the horses, grazing peacefully. Luckily his approach had been downwind or Anna's horses would have smelled his. As it was, the little scene in the valley looked awfully quiet.

Anna was nowhere in sight, and he continued to search for her. She had to be nearby. She would never have left her horses alone.

Movement on the edge of the river caught his attention and he focused the binoculars there. His heart slammed hard against his ribs as he watched a tall, slender woman—dark hair dripping a curtain of water—climb up onto a rock. She was completely naked and seemed absolutely comfortable with her lack of clothing.

He held his breath until he thought his lungs would burst. Anna dove back into the river. It was a beautiful, controlled dive that revealed every inch of her perfect body.

Jeremy fought against the sensations that seemed to hit him with the force of a lightning bolt. He was a man who loved women, and he was always aware of their beauty. But he'd never had a reaction like the one Anna evoked.

He desired her. But he also held her in a certain awe. She was so much a part of the landscape. She belonged to the water of the Guadeloupe and the sun and the rocks in a way that he could only envy.

Jeremy wasn't certain whether it was desire or envy

that made him short of wind and dizzy. He lowered the binoculars and tried to rein in his imagination.

During the long, hot hours of tracking Anna Red Shoes he'd anticipated all kinds of trouble. He'd played out scenarios in which he had to lasso her and point a gun at her. Now all he wanted to do was kiss her—run his hands over her skin, now slick with water. He could almost feel the span of her slender waist, the swell of her hips.

He leaned back against a rock and closed his eyes. This was the woman who'd killed his friend and editor, Henry Mills. And he was having sexual fantasies about her. What was wrong with him?

He had to gain control of himself and the situation. He'd come all this way to do a job—his future depended on the way he handled this predicament. The only answer was for him to do what he'd come to do— take Anna back to the law.

His grip on the rifle tightened. He had several choices. He could send a few bullets into the river near Anna and frighten her good. That way she'd know he was armed and meant business. Or he could sneak up on her and take the up-close-and-personal approach.

He made his decision. Moving stealthily, he eased down to the river. Though it would put more of a personal strain on him, it was the safest bet in taking her prisoner. Anna would be distracted by the noise of the river.

He made it down to the river and quickly gathered up her clothes. Next he went to her horses. Releasing the hobbles, he slapped them on the rump and sent them running away. He'd just ducked behind a tree trunk, when Anna popped out of the water. She obviously heard the sound of hooves, and there was an expression of doubt and then despair as she watched her horses flee.

The expression that crossed her face next was one of wariness. She looked all around.

Jeremy could almost read her thoughts. She'd finally figured out that someone had taken the hobbles off the horses. Now she was looking for that someone.

He didn't move as she crept up the rocky bank and eased from one rock to the next, slowly approaching her campsite and the place where she'd left her clothes.

The look of consternation on her face when she realized her clothes were missing was almost comic. But what happened next made his heart slam hard into his ribs for the second time.

Anna gave up her crouching position and stood tall and regal. ''Whoever you are, come on out and face me,'' she said, throwing down the challenge without a weapon or a stitch of clothes.

Jeremy was mesmerized. He couldn't look away from her, and what he saw was a proud woman who refused to yield to fear or danger.

In that moment, he knew that he had never met anyone quite like Anna Red Shoes—and he felt a rush of regret that they were enemies.

Chapter Five

Out in the open, Anna felt colder than she had in the icy water. The sun was warm, but the idea that someone was watching her sent shivers down her spine. Her horses had galloped only three hundred yards away, but they might as well have been in Canada.

Her clothes were also gone, which meant that the person who'd turned her horses free was somewhere very close. Watching. The idea was frightening.

She had never felt so vulnerable, but she refused to show her fear. Her grandfather had taught her that to show fear was to invite tragedy. *"You carry the blood of warriors,"* he'd told her. *"Always remember it. Never bow in fear."*

Heeding those long-remembered words and the pride that had never abandoned her grandfather, Anna stood straighter. She cleared her throat. "Whatever you want, tell me. Perhaps we can negotiate."

It crossed her mind that someone from the posse might have caught up with her, but she dismissed that idea. It simply wasn't possible. Even taking into account her nap and the fifteen minutes in the river, there was no way Jeremy Masterson or any of his cohorts could have closed in on her that fast.

One thing nagged at her: whomever was out there could have taken her horses, her gear and everything else. But her material possessions obviously weren't what he or they were after. Anna didn't like the other images that flickered through her mind, but she also refused to allow her imagination to cripple her.

"Whoever you are, come out and talk," she said calmly.

When the tall man stepped out from behind the tree, she almost didn't recognize Jeremy. The sun was behind him, putting his features into silhouette. When she finally realized who he was, she simply stared. He was like a vision—one of the old spirits her grandfather had warned her about.

Thunder Horse had often told her that there were unhappy spirits that roamed the earth looking for a human to attach to. Once the attachment was made, the spirit was very difficult to shake.

"How did you get free so fast?" she asked in a tone that showed she still doubted her eyes.

"Never underestimate a Texan," he said slowly.

She was aware that he kept looking away from her. His gaze would flick up to her eyes and then drop away. She knew instantly—and with a strange sensation—that he was attracted to her body, and he didn't want to acknowledge it. She filed the information away in case she needed it later. Another lesson she'd learned from her grandfather was that a man was only as strong as his greatest weakness. Jeremy Masterson loved women. She knew that from his writing and from his behavior. It wasn't a trump she wanted to play, but it was one she'd use if she had to.

"May I have my clothes?" she asked.

"Sure," he said, "but first you have to promise me that you won't try to escape."

Anna almost didn't believe her ears. Almost. Then again, considering the source, anything was possible. "You want to barter my clothes for a promise that I'll follow you back to town like a sheep to the slaughter? I'm sorry, but where did you grow up?"

He nodded. "You're not exactly in a position to dictate terms," he pointed out as he held up her clothes.

"Forget it." She turned away and sat down in the grass. The sun felt warm on her water-chilled body, and though she was intensely aware of Jeremy's hot gaze, she refused to look at him.

Jeremy stood for a moment. "If you want to ride back to Kerrville as naked as the day you were born, that's fine with me," he said. "But you're going back."

Anna almost wanted to laugh. It obviously wasn't fine with him, but he didn't know what to do about it. She had learned something else about him. He was an arrogant man, but he didn't enjoy the role of bully. She'd forced him to a place he didn't like, and he was going to try to bluff his way out.

"I'm not going anywhere," she said, not bothering to look at him—a little afraid to look at him. Knowing that he was looking at her with such undisguised desire made her ill-at-ease. Though he was a liar, she was not immune to him.

"We're going back to Kerrville. The posse is only a couple of hours behind me." He patted his foot. "It would be better for you if you went peacefully."

"I'm perfectly happy right here." As bold as she sounded, Anna knew she was in a real jam. Jeremy wasn't going to be taken by surprise twice. And though she wasn't looking directly at him, she had seen enough to know that he was determined to take her back.

"You can stay there until you dry out," he said, easing down on one heel, cowboy-style. "I need a little rest myself, and my horses are worn down." He glanced toward the sun, which was hanging above the treetops. "There's no way we'll make it back today, anyway." He grinned. "We might as well camp here. A night out under the stars might make you more reasonable."

Anna hadn't expected such sanguine behavior. She glanced at her clothes, still clutched tightly in his hands. He noticed, and she caught the hint of amusement in his eyes.

He thought he had her! It was completely infuriating. In fact, sitting out on the banks of a river, naked with Jeremy Masterson, was beginning to get to her. Anna had a lot of self-control, but she didn't know if she could keep herself from blushing.

He'd caught her by surprise, and she'd reacted as her grandfather had taught her. But Thunder Horse had never given her advice on how to handle the situation that now confronted her. She wanted her clothes!

As if he read her mind, Jeremy tossed her the damp flannel shirt and her underwear.

Anna snatched them, then glared at him until he turned his back and gave her the privacy to put them on. Her dry pants were going to be held hostage, she realized, but the shirt was enough to cover her. Once she had slipped into the flannel, she began to cast around for a plan.

"Don't get any ideas," Jeremy said.

She turned to face him, and saw that he was watching her as if he were trying to figure her out.

"I didn't kill your editor," she said. She knew she'd caught him by surprise, but then she saw his features harden.

"Tell it to the sheriff."

"You know as well as I do that once they have me for a suspect, they won't look any farther."

Jeremy walked over to the place where she'd left her boots. He picked one up and examined it. "There were some prints exactly the size—"

"Okay, I went into your home," she said, knowing that it would be pointless to deny it. "I went to talk to you. I saw the body and I thought it was you. I thought you'd had a heart attack or something, and I went inside to help you."

She could see that he didn't believe a word she said. "I'm telling you the truth," she said. "I don't expect you to believe me, but it is the truth."

"You sneaked through a window. How do you think that makes you look?" He let that sit with her a moment. "Why were you peeping in the window?"

Anna took a slow breath. He was at least asking a question. This was progress, of a sort. If he would just listen. If he would just look in her eyes he could see the truth. "I went to the door and rang the bell and knocked. No one answered. I saw the glare of a light and I thought you might be up, working late." She hesitated. "Then I went to look in. I thought even if you wouldn't talk to me, I would see you…at work."

Nothing in his face changed, but she could sense a difference in the way he was looking at her.

"Are you telling me that you wanted to see me at work…because you've read my books?"

There was no going back now. Anna held her head up. "I thought you were the finest writer Texas had ever produced. Until your latest book."

"You're a fan?" Jeremy asked in a voice devoid of emotion.

"I was," she admitted. "And I was still fan enough to walk to that window. I knew it was wrong, but I didn't see what it could really hurt—one tiny little peek. And if you were in there writing, I was going to tap on the window and get your attention. I'd already decided you probably wouldn't listen to my side of the story, but I had to make one last attempt. I'd written my points down and I was going to leave them for you."

She found herself staring into his blue eyes. Deep-blue eyes that seemed, at least for the moment, to be paying attention only to her. "There are two reasons I had to try again. My grandfather was a great man, a kind man who deserves to be painted with the truth, not with convenient lies." She looked down at her toes in the green grass.

"And the second reason?" Jeremy asked.

"It's hard to give up a hero," she said softly, looking up at him.

There was a long silence, and Anna dropped her gaze before he did. She'd admitted far more than she had ever intended.

"So you saw the body?" he pressed, choosing to ignore the personal nature of her revelation.

She concentrated on remembering. "I didn't know it was a dead person. I thought it was you. I tapped on the window, and you didn't respond. That's when I thought you might be in trouble."

She looked up, found his gaze again and held it. "I

could have driven off. Instead, I cut the screen and went inside. I intended to help if I could.''

"And then what happened?"

Anna didn't look away from him. "I touched the body and knew the man was dead. I went back out the window and came back to my camp."

"Why didn't you call the authorities?"

Anna shook her head. "I'd broken into your house and there was a dead man there. Had I called the sheriff, I would be in jail now, instead of here."

"It would have looked better for you."

"That's what you say. If I hadn't gone into the bookstore and made a threat against you, that might be true. But as the facts stand now, I would have been accused of the murder no matter what I'd done. I hoped only to get back to my camp and then return home. I should have known it was a stupid hope. The arm of the law is long, especially against certain people. Like me."

Jeremy walked to her and dropped the jeans in her lap. "I'll gather some firewood to build a fire. We might as well get comfortable. We'll break camp at sunrise and head back. We should meet the posse, and from what I can hear, there's a bunch of media with them."

"I see," Anna said. And she did. It was going to be a great tabloid story. The wild, wild West rides again. Cowboys and Indians. Famous author against crazy female. There were a million angles from which to play it, none of them even close to the heart of the matter. That was the thing about history—it was re-played again and again. She would be the villain because of her heritage. Once the media got the story, there wouldn't even be an attempt at justice.

Chances were that Jeremy had called the media before he even came after her. The publicity would push
his book sales to the number one place on the bestseller list.

"We'll try to avoid them," Jeremy said.

Surprised, she glanced up at him. "Why?"

"This isn't my idea of fun," he said. "I came after
you because I believe you killed Henry. That's the
only reason."

"I'm sure the idea of the publicity is total anathema
to you." She couldn't keep the scathing note from her
voice.

"More than you might imagine." He picked up a
few branches from beneath the trees by the riverbank.
Working methodically he stacked them for a fire. "Do
you know Blane Griffin?"

"The author?" Anna knew him. He was a writer
she considered pedestrian. He did the same characters
and story again and again.

"He's on the posse. He's the one who set up the
press conferences."

Anna could tell there was more between Jeremy and
Blane than just writing. Professional jealousy? A
woman? Blane was also a handsome man, and one
who liked to flaunt his machismo. The two men would
be like roosters in a henhouse.

"You could avoid the whole mess and let me go,"
she suggested.

Jeremy didn't answer. Instead, he stacked the wood
he'd quickly gathered and knelt down to light the fire.
Dusk was coming on fast. He worked quickly and ef-
ficiently, like a real woodsman. Anna watched his
hands. They were strong, callused. Not the hands of a

writer but the hands of a man. Her skin tingled at the thought, and she forced it out of her mind.

The fire was small but hot, and Anna felt the need to move a little closer to it. Instead, she picked up her jeans and slid into them.

"You want me to feed your horses?" he asked.

"I'll do it." She stood up, then looked pointedly at her boots.

Jeremy's eyebrows quirked. "Give me your word that you won't try to escape."

Anna wanted to slug him. "Why would the word of a woman you think is a murderer be of any use to you?" she asked.

"It's always a good policy," he said. "If you're honorable, you'll respect your word. If you aren't, then it hasn't hurt to try."

"I need my boots," she said.

"Sorry. Your word, first."

Anna wanted to give him a word—one he wouldn't forget. "I'll make you a promise that I won't do anything tonight," she said. That was hardly a concession, since she wouldn't risk running her horses in the dark. To have any hope of getting away, she needed daylight.

Jeremy's eyes were silvery mirrors that hid his thoughts. "Good," he said. He picked up her boots and brought them to her, along with her socks. "This way it'll be a lot easier for both of us."

Anna accepted her boots, with their worn, soft leather. But her fingers brushed against his hard ones as she took them. The touch was electric, and they both froze.

"We need more firewood," he said, then abruptly turned and walked toward the setting sun.

JEREMY STRETCHED his long legs as far as they would go, putting as much distance as possible between himself and Anna Red Shoes. It was insane, but he'd wanted to take the woman in his arms and kiss her. This rush of desire had to have everything to do with her glorious former nakedness and his months of abstinence. That had to be the reason, he argued with himself as he loaded his arms with wood.

His desire for her was perfectly natural—the reaction of one healthy human to another. It had nothing to do with her fearlessness or her pride or her spirit. She was a beautiful woman, exactly the kind he fantasized about. Tall, willowy, long dark hair—and she'd stepped out of the river like some Texan Aphrodite. If he hadn't felt the stirrings of desire, he would have been seriously worried about himself. One thing was certain, though. He was in control of the situation.

He worked at a furious pace, but always kept one eye on Anna. She sat before the fire, her face in profile to him. Her dark hair was sleek and black in the slanting light of the dying day. She was as still as a statue.

Jeremy had enough wood, but he lingered beneath the cottonwoods and let the gurgle of the river calm him. Despite his intentions, he couldn't keep his gaze away from Anna.

She wasn't like any other woman he'd ever known. She was so completely herself, so whole. And so damn proud. She'd come out of that river as if she had an M-16 and a battalion behind her. It was a moment that would live forever in his memory, and his imagination.

That was the trouble—his damn imagination. He had no difficulty at all imagining what it would feel like to touch her skin. He could almost feel it now, beneath his fingertips. Smooth and soft. He could tell just by looking at her.

And her hair—it hung like heavy silk. The texture would be like rippling water in his hands.

And her lips. He had studied them while she talked. Full, passionate. She would be a woman who put herself into a kiss. She would be as fearless in her decision to love as she was in facing an enemy.

That thought almost made him drop the firewood.

He also realized that although he was in control of his actions, his imagination was running wild and free. Something about Anna unleashed his mind and led him into passions that were better kept strictly off-limits. He'd known lots of beautiful, tempting women, but none had ever affected him the way Anna did.

In coming after her alone, he had made the first in a series of errors. The biggest one, though, was that he hadn't taken into account how attractive she was. Or how he would react to her. He'd always prided himself on being the one in control in any relationship. It had never occurred to him that he would find this woman desirable.

Anna Red Shoes had very probably killed his editor. She denied it, of course, but criminals always denied the crime.

Yet…he remembered her eyes, so dark and so damn sincere. He'd been on the verge of believing her when she'd said she was innocent.

What he had to focus on was bringing Anna back to justice. If she was innocent—and there was a part of him that believed, or wanted to believe, she might be—then a jury would find her so. All his life he'd believed in the justice system. He couldn't waver now. The only trouble was, there were certain people who *hadn't* received justice, the Native Americans among them.

But that was the past. Things were different now. He had to hold on to that belief.

"Are you bringing more wood or have you gotten lost?" Anna called out.

He was amazed that she could joke at a time like this. He started back to the fire. He had to tend to business. If he kept his mind on what he had to do, the night would pass and soon they would be back in Kerrville. Then Anna would no longer be his problem.

In silence, he built up the fire and brought cans of food out of his pack. Anna, too, worked without speaking as she opened the cans, got out cooking utensils and arranged the food around the fire to heat. She was an accomplished camper.

"I'll re-hobble the horses," he offered.

"No, thanks. They know me." She stood and picked up the hobbles, walking into the near darkness. When she was away from the fire she whistled, and both mares came running to her.

Jeremy was suitably impressed with her horse-handling skills, too. Anna was a woman who definitely left an impression, in more ways than one.

She'd just finished hobbling Allegro, when her mares and Jeremy's horses lifted their heads. They turned into the wind, nostrils flaring.

Jeremy reached for his rifle and started toward Anna, but she was gone. He hadn't even seen her move. For a split second he felt a roar of disappointment. She'd given her word. Well, that showed what her word was worth. While he was at the river, mooning over her like some high school dope, she'd been planning her escape.

"Jeremy!" Her voice was soft yet insistent. "Over here," she called.

He saw her then, a darker shadow against the outline of a large tree. She waved him low to the ground and spoke softly yet with urgency. "Get down!"

He obeyed by instinct, working his way over to her.

"There's someone up on the ridge," she said as soon as he was beside her.

He looked toward the east. The horses were behaving strangely—that was true. There could be someone up there.

Jeremy felt a stiletto of doubt. If there was a person up on the ridge, it might well be someone Anna was expecting. She'd been awfully calm about being caught. Maybe she'd known all along that rescue was imminent.

He felt her against him, the light rise of her chest as she breathed. She was staring into the night as if she, too, were wary of whoever was up there.

"Did you see anyone?" he asked.

"No." She pointed. "Right there, I think. How far behind you was the posse?"

Jeremy calculated. The only way someone from the posse could have arrived so soon was if they'd known where they were going all along.

"Too far behind."

"Who is it, then?" she asked, her voice hollow.

He didn't have an answer. There was the sound of a rock slipping up on the crest of the hill. The echo was stark in the still night. Above the ridge the stars had begun to spring out of the velvet sky. In a few hours the moon would rise and they would have a better chance.

But in a few hours, Jeremy knew, it might be too late.

Chapter Six

Anna was keenly aware of Jeremy beside her. He was tensed, ready for action. Though the contact between them was minimal, she could feel the muscles in his leg and shoulder pressing against her as he crouched with her behind the rock.

She refocused her attention on the ridge about a hundred yards away. She'd been so preoccupied with Jeremy that she'd let her guard down. Someone had sneaked up on them, and she hadn't had a clue. She wasn't using the skills she'd been trained to use.

Now she had to figure out who it was and what they wanted—before she jumped to the wrong conclusion.

The most logical assumption was that someone from the posse had followed Jeremy. The rugged country around Kerrville had produced many skilled trackers and riders—people who knew the terrain and shortcuts.

If the person up on the hill was from the posse, Anna knew, her luck had just run out. Jeremy was enough of a challenge. With two guarding her, the opportunities to escape would be few to none.

"I'm going up after them," Jeremy said.

Without thinking, Anna put a hand on his arm. The

thought flashed across her mind that if this person was from the posse, Jeremy would not *need* to meet him. Her sixth sense warned of danger, and she reacted instinctively. "Don't. They've seen us. They know where we are. Let them make the first move."

In the instant that she touched him, she knew her attempt to protect him had failed. He was going to do the opposite of what she suggested. In his position, she might have done the same.

When he darted out from behind the rock, she didn't say anything. He was a man who was going to do things his way, whether it was sensible or not.

She heard his progress as he moved from tree to boulder, heading up the south side of the ridge. The horses had shifted closer to her. Anna spoke softly, soothing them. She tried not to think about the possible consequences of Jeremy's actions.

If it wasn't someone from the posse, it was probably only a harmless camper. This was modern Texas. Desperados and killers weren't hiding out behind every stand of scrub cedar. Rangers with hair-trigger guns weren't looking for renegades and murderers. Still, she couldn't calm the anxiety that surged with every beat of her heart.

By her calculations, Jeremy had gained the ridge. Now there was no sound from that direction. The silence was ominous.

Beside her, one of the horses snorted wildly. Air blew out of its nostrils in a sharp expression of fear. Anna had no time to worry about Jeremy. She slipped from behind her protection and went to the animals. Hobbled, they couldn't run. And it was a good thing they were hobbled. Anna could tell by the way they were trembling and blowing that flight was the only thing on their minds.

"Easy," she whispered. "Easy."

Anna had hardly finished speaking when the cry of a big cat stretched across the night—a long wail of danger and fury.

"Mountain lion," she said aloud. She recognized the animal's raw voice. The big cats were rare in Hill Country—most killed by ranchers and pseudo big-game hunters—but they weren't extinct. She held her breath and waited.

The low, throbbing cry came again, this time edged with what sounded like anger. Anna's grandfather had taught her to listen to the language of the wild animals. Thunder Horse, a man who'd been hunted like a wild animal, had always believed in giving a cornered creature his say. Often, a confrontation could be avoided. Anna thought of Jeremy, and knew he wasn't the kind of man to listen—not to her, and not to a cat.

The night seemed to vibrate with the big cat's roar. Anna knew what was happening almost as if she were at the scene. The lion was standing his ground, refusing to be pushed away from what he viewed as his next meal—one of the hobbled horses.

Anna left the trembling horses and ran toward the fire. There had been a rifle in Jeremy's saddle. Had he taken it? She didn't know. But if it was there, she wanted it.

The danger on the ridge was not human. It had been the lion that the horses had sensed and been frightened by. They'd known long before she did that a predator was stalking them.

Fumbling in the darkness, she found Jeremy's saddle and her fingers closed over the stock of the rifle.

She pulled it free, checked to make sure it was loaded, and turned toward the ridge.

"Jeremy?" she called out.

Her voice carried clearly on the still night air.

There was no answer.

"Jeremy?" she called more loudly. "I've got the rifle. I can come up and help you."

"Stay with the horses," he called back.

She couldn't get a clear reading on where he was. It sounded as if he'd traveled north along the ridge. And there was something strange about his voice.

"Have you seen the lion?" She hoped the sound of a second human would be enough to drive the predator away. Mountain lions seldom attacked a man. Seldom.

"Stay with the horses," Jeremy repeated, and there was that tone in his voice that made Anna start forward immediately. Hefting the gun in one hand, she ran toward the ridge.

It took her ten minutes of scrabbling over the loose rocks before she heard a soft curse.

"Damn it all to hell, I told you to stay with the horses."

In the bright starlight, she finally located Jeremy. He was sitting against a rock. She didn't need more light to determine that he was injured.

"What happened?" she asked, going to him. She put the gun down beside his leg as she leaned in closer. The smell of blood struck her instantly. Her hand went to his leg, and she felt the warm stickiness.

"The cat was hidden under a ledge." There was an undercurrent of pain in his voice as he paused for breath. "When I went by, he took a swipe at me. A pretty accurate swipe. I used that branch—" he pointed to a long, broken limb "—to hold him off. He must have been more afraid of me than hungry. But he's hunting. If he doesn't find other game, he may be back.''

Anna could do little with the wound until she was able to see it. What she did know was that he'd lost a lot of blood. She could feel it pooling around his leg on the ground. ''We have to get off this ridge and back to the camp,'' she said. She didn't have to tell him that the rocks and crags of the ridge made a perfect place for the cat to hide and ambush them.

''I can get one of the horses, but first I need to make sure the lion is gone,'' she said. She worked as she talked. She slipped out of her shirt, aware that Jeremy watched her actions. She tore the sleeves out of the soft old flannel, slipped back into the shirt and then tied the sleeves together.

She wrapped the tourniquet around his upper thigh and knotted it. Then she found a strong stick, inserted it into the band of material and tightened until he gasped.

''You've lost a lot of blood,'' she said. ''Can you manage this?''

In answer, he took the stick from her and held it steady.

''I'll be back,'' she promised. She knew if she didn't return, he would die.

Jeremy's hand caught her wrist. She thought for a moment that he was going to try to restrain her. He knew that at this moment his life was in her hands. There was nothing to prevent her from going down the ridge, saddling her horses and riding away. No one could possibly hold her responsible for the death of a man who was attacked by a wildcat.

''Be careful,'' he said. ''The cat's smart and he's

determined. Most wild animals would have fled. I don't think he intends to leave until he's eaten.'' His grip tightened. "And he doesn't care if his supper is one of the horses or one of us.''

Anna took a deep breath. "He's only trying to survive, Jeremy.'' It was the first time she'd spoken his name in conversation, and it made her stomach tighten. "When you push a living creature—man or animal—into a confrontation, someone always gets hurt. Sometimes there's no place left to back up.''

Anna picked up the rifle and started after the cat.

JEREMY WATCHED Anna walk away. She held the rifle with confidence and skill. She'd do what she had to do to protect them and the horses. Even if she didn't want to.

He knew that was exactly the point she was making. Jeremy wasn't stupid. She'd drawn a very neat parallel between her grandfather and the mountain lion. Both endangered. Both hunted relentlessly. Both trying only to survive.

To make her point, she'd taken the rifle and gone to do the job she clearly didn't want to do.

Jeremy used his hands to push up, and felt the fire in his leg shoot up his spine to his brain. To keep from thinking about his wound and the dangerous cat—and the possible repercussions that now faced them—he thought about Anna.

He'd never known a woman so unaware of her physical beauty. He was used to women who led with their charms. When she'd taken off her shirt, it had been an act of necessity. She was doing the most practical thing to save his life. She'd never given a thought to the fact that the sight of her smooth skin, her breasts revealed in the moonlight, might move him. To Jeremy, her naiveté was just an added bit of excitement.

He wondered what motivated her. Pride? Insanity? It could be either. She had a ticket to freedom in her hand. All she had to do was saddle up and ride into the night.

For some strange reason, he knew she wouldn't. She wouldn't leave him alone on the ridge, wounded, with a predator somewhere close by. How did he know this? That was a question that he had to answer. Especially in light of the fact that he'd come after her because he thought she'd killed a man in cold blood.

Jeremy shifted position again, knowing that his thoughts as much as his wound were making him uncomfortable.

If he was wrong about Anna, was he also wrong about Thunder Horse?

He'd worked on his book for two years. He'd read every bit of history he could lay his hands on. He'd interviewed the relatives of survivors and taken copious notes. Was it possible that he'd done everything he knew to do and had still gotten it wrong?

The one thing that niggled—a tiny little buzz saw of aggravation—was that he hadn't attempted to search out any of Thunder Horse's relatives. He'd done his extensive research only with the white settlers. And the real crime was that he'd never thought to look up any of the Natives.

"Damnation," he said, shifting again. The resulting pain in his leg was a lot more acceptable than the distress his thoughts were causing.

The cry of the lion cut off any further brooding. The savage, furious roar had Jeremy on his feet and hobbling toward the sound. Anna was skilled, no doubt about it. But he couldn't allow her to face that cat alone.

Pain from the wound made him dizzy, and he leaned against a rock. Some help *he* was going to be. He was as helpless as an infant—a fact he hated.

Gathering his strength, he forced himself to stand and continue walking. This time, when the cat's long wail came, it was from the back of the ridge.

The animal was moving away.

Jeremy knew his face was covered in sweat though the night was cool. His attempt to walk had cost him greatly, in strength and in reserve. He slowly sank against a rock, relieved that, at least for the moment, the cat had decided to retreat. And Anna hadn't fired a single shot.

It was then that he heard the *clop* of a horse's shod hoof on the solid rock of the ridge.

"Jeremy?" Anna called out, concern evident.

"Here," he said, wishing he'd stayed where she'd left him. He didn't have the strength to get back there.

Anna led the horse to him—one of hers, he noticed. The Appaloosa. The animal held steady while she helped Jeremy mount. She said nothing about the fact that he'd gotten up and walked. Not a word.

"If you feel dizzy, say so," she said matter-of-factly as she began to lead the horse toward the camp-site. "I realize you're macho and very stubborn, but if you fall off the horse and crack your skull open, I'll leave you."

She didn't even bother to turn around as she gave her edict. Jeremy felt the surge of anger, and then he chuckled. She was baiting him, getting him riled, knowing that the rush of adrenaline would give him enough strength to hang on for what was going to be a painful ride.

And she was right. As the horse began to slip and slide down the ridge, he felt every jolt, every movement. It was all he could do to keep his grip on the saddle horn—and his mouth shut.

ANNA KEPT A CLOSE watch on Jeremy as they made their way back to the relative safety of the camp. She tried to do it subtly, knowing how delicate a man's ego could be. Still, by the time they reached the flat land by the river, she was afraid he was going to topple off the horse.

How she would ever help him dismount without breaking something was a bridge she'd have to cross soon enough. She was strong, but he was a big man.

''We're here,'' she said as she halted Allegro by the dying embers of the fire. She needed more wood. Hot water was going to be required to clean his wound.

''Okay.''

His voice was too soft. Anna dropped the reins and went to him. The wound was on his right leg, which should have made dismounting easier. But the trip down the ridge, though not a long distance, had taken a lot of his strength.

''Come on, Jeremy,'' she said, patting his leg. ''Lean on my shoulder.''

Somehow they managed. She supported his weight as best she could, easing him down by the fire. His body felt chilled to her—a bad sign. If he went into shock, there was little she could do for him. He needed a doctor.

Using her sleeping bag, she made him as warm and comfortable as possible, and then began gathering wood, water and the tools necessary to try to clean out the wound. The bleeding had stopped. Now she feared infection. That and weakness could take down the strongest man.

She tried not to think about her options. It had crossed her mind to leave him. She was not so honorable as not to have contemplated the act. But she couldn't bring herself to do it. Now she knew she was trapped. Unless he had a lot more strength than she anticipated, he wouldn't be able to ride for at least two days. And he wouldn't be able to care for himself.

Which meant she'd be sitting at the campfire, tending him, when the posse arrived to arrest her.

She bit her lip at the irony of the situation. She was accused of killing a man, and she would be caught because she couldn't allow one to die. It wasn't exactly the fairest of circumstances. But when had she ever expected fairness?

"Anna?"

She was surprised at his voice. She'd been so busy with her thoughts that she'd forgotten he was conscious. It would be better for him if he were not.

She went back to the campfire, which had grown brighter with the wood she'd supplied. In the dancing flames she could see his features. He was weak but lucid.

"How did you get the lion to leave?" he asked. "You didn't fire a shot."

"I didn't want to frighten the horses," she said. "Or alert the posse, if they were near."

"So how did you get it to leave?"

"I made him understand that I had no choice but to kill him if he didn't move on."

She saw disbelief cross his face.

"I told you earlier. Sometimes you have to listen to know the truth. The lion was willing to listen." She sat beside him with the supplies she needed to clean the wound. "This is going to hurt, and there's nothing I can do to help you. Tomorrow, I'll look for some plants. Tonight—" she shrugged "—I can't see well enough."

She brought out her pocketknife and made a move toward his leg. His hand stopped her abruptly.

"You think after getting you off the ridge I'd do something now?" she asked, not bothering to disguise the anger in her voice. He was like so many others. Stupid.

"Wait," he said. "Tomorrow, leave me the gun and go on."

Anna almost didn't believe what she was hearing. "You want me to leave you?"

He nodded.

"You've lost a lot of blood. You—"

"That's not your problem," he said. "I want you to go on. They'll find me, and I'll be fine."

"What if they don't?"

"I'm hurt, but I'm not about to die."

She pondered his words. "Why are you doing this?"

"Because I'm not sure. There's a chance I was wrong and you're right."

She rocked back on her heels and stared into his eyes. In the moonlight she couldn't be certain of what she saw there.

"I didn't kill that man in your house."

Jeremy nodded slowly. "I don't think you did."

Anna felt the strangest sensation. It was part relief, but also something else. She had the strongest impulse to reach out to Jeremy, to put her hand on him to make sure that he wasn't so fevered he didn't know what he was saying.

"You think running is my smartest move?" she finally asked.

Jeremy hesitated before he spoke again. "Three hours ago I would have said no. But the more I think about this, the more I realize that I've led a lot of people to believe you're guilty. I need a chance to convince them otherwise." He took a breath. "I thought about what you said. If they have you in custody, they might not look to find the real killer. I came after you because I wanted to avenge the death of Henry Mills. I want the killer caught and punished. If you're right—if they arrest you—the real killer will never be caught."

It was a long speech for a man who was suffering so intensely. Anna took it all in. She'd never believed that Jeremy Masterson would allow a chink in his armor of self-righteousness.

Obviously she'd underestimated the man. Not only had he listened to her, he'd thought about what she said and come to his own conclusions. Now he was offering to do the best he could to right matters, at the risk of his own life.

"We'll see how you are in the morning," she said, knowing now that she couldn't abandon him.

"I'm giving you an opportunity to escape," he said, his voice rough now with the strain of talking.

"I'm not turning it down," Anna said evenly. "I'm saying, we'll see how things stand in the morning." She slit his pants leg with a motion so smooth and practiced that he didn't have time to protest.

"You said I was hardheaded," Jeremy accused. "You're every bit as bad. Or worse."

"There's no point worrying about what I'll do in the morning," she said, knowing her tone would anger him. "You might well be dead."

"Dead!" he sputtered.

"I don't know for sure," she added. "But I do know one thing. Once I start cleaning this wound, you'll think death is a blessing. Now grit your teeth and let me do what I have to do."

Chapter Seven

Anna leaned back against the saddle and tried to relax her shoulders. She was exhausted. Jeremy, thank goodness, was finally asleep. He'd hung tough throughout the entire process of cleaning his wound. The pain would have sent a weaker man into unconsciousness.

The cat's wicked claws had raked long and deep up the muscle of his calf, but to Anna's amazement, it wasn't as bad as it could have been. The bone had not been exposed. She'd pulled the wound together as best she could and bound it.

Tomorrow, there were herbs she could find that would work better than the tube of antibiotic salve she'd packed in her saddlebag. But she feared that Jeremy needed a doctor and antibiotics. The herbal cures she knew about were more folklore than fact.

Maria Gonzalez could help him. She was a nurse, and a skillful one. But they were a long way from the haven of her ranch.

Jeremy moaned and shifted, and she went to him. Before modern medicine, men had survived such attacks. She tried to bolster her own courage with that thought. Her grandfather had been a leader, not a medicine man, but he had known one of the greatest of all healers, Golden Bear.

Anna found a comfortable position where she could watch Jeremy and keep an eye on the campfire. It was burning low and steady, but the night was still cold— cold enough that she was worried about the wounded man. He was already weakened from his ordeal. Shivering all night would only make it worse.

To keep the fear at bay, she returned to thoughts of Golden Bear. He was one of the wisest of all the Natives in the Texas territory.

It was said that on the day he was born, a large bear had come out of the hills just at daybreak, when the sun was huge and golden on the horizon. Somehow the animal had slipped past all the warriors and walked into the main area of the Native camp.

Of course, all the women and children were terrified. Mothers snatched babies and began to run, but Yellow Feather, Golden Bear's mother, was too weak from childbirth to run.

She cradled her newborn infant in her arms and struggled out of her teepee right into the path of the bear. They stood looking at each other.

The bear reared up on his hind legs, and all the Natives watching were sure that it was going to swipe Yellow Feather and her baby with one huge paw. Instead, the huge beast roared. It roared three times with its mighty voice. Framed by the morning sun, it looked as if it were made of gold to those who were watching the terrifying scene.

Then, without another sound, the bear turned away and went back to the woods. But everyone knew that the infant Yellow Feather held in her arms was a special child. The bear had come to view the baby. So the name Golden Bear was given to the child, and he did indeed grow to be a wise man with the touch of healing that only the gods could bestow.

Anna found herself smiling at the story. She could hear her grandfather's voice. He had been a wonderful storyteller, and she had always believed every story he told.

Now she had to have faith that Golden Bear's remedies might help Jeremy. She knew the herbs the Natives had used for healing. She'd learned them to please her grandfather. Now she would apply that knowledge. As soon as dawn broke, she'd find some and make a salve for Jeremy's leg.

Jeremy shifted restlessly, and she went to him again, touching his forehead. His skin was cool. No fever. Just the opposite: he was cold. And she was, too. She'd given him her sleeping bag as well as his blanket. In her now sleeveless shirt and a jacket, she shivered.

No matter how close to the fire she got, she couldn't get warm. Her hand drifted to Jeremy's face, the stubble of his beard rough against her palm, his mustache surprisingly soft as the ends of it teased her fingers.

His eyes opened and he looked at her. "I'm cold," he whispered, and his teeth chattered slightly.

"I'll put more wood on the fire," she said, starting to rise.

His hand caught hers and held, a firm grip. "You're cold, too."

Anna was surprised at his lucidity. "I'll be fine."

"I don't doubt that you could survive the sinking of the Titanic. That's not the point. Get under the sleeping bag with me. We can keep each other warm."

It was a sensible suggestion. Anna had considered it—fleetingly—and then rejected it.

"I'm fine right here," she said.

His grip tightened slightly. "Anna, I won't bite you. I'm cold and so are you. You've given me your sleeping bag. If you won't share with me, then you take it back."

She knew that was ridiculous. He couldn't afford such a gesture.

"Please," he said softly.

Of all the words she'd thought to hear pass Jeremy Masterson's lips, *please* was not one of them. She found herself moving to the far side and slipping beneath the cover. The warmth of his body was like a magnet, and she moved close enough to touch him without pressing against him.

"Better?" he asked.

"Yes," she admitted. It was far better. She could already feel the tension in her muscles begin to lessen. Now, maybe she could catch a few hours of sleep. She hadn't realized how tired she was.

"Anna?" She felt him shift as he turned to face her.

"Don't move around too much," she cautioned him. "Your leg is held together by good intentions. If you twist too much, you could open it again."

"Okay." He settled against her more firmly, his hip brushing hers, his uninjured leg pressed against the length of her leg. "Can I ask you something?"

She stared up at the stars. "Okay."

"If you didn't kill Henry Mills, who do you think did? I found the knife. It was yours. The one from the book signing."

Anna's first reaction was to say that such a thing

was impossible. She looked up in the sky at the constellation known as the Seven Sisters. "I left the knife at the bookstore. You know that. I was so angry I forgot it. As for who might want to harm Henry Mills, or you, I don't really know anything about your life. I can't even guess." She had a thought. "Where did you go after the book signing?"

"To the Ketterings. Friends who held a party for me. I helped set up—well, really I just relaxed." He hit the ground with a fist. "Dammit. That was after I drove out to Ray Moody's to look at some cattle. It was on the way, and I was thinking about buying some of the longhorns he breeds."

"Did he see you?" Anna asked the question casually.

"No. I didn't go up to the house. The herd was up in the hills, and I wanted some solitude. I walked over the property." He paused. "I've been giving it some thought. The people who knew Henry was at my house were Ellie…and the people at the book signing who might have overheard us talking about him. Oh, and the people at the party, including Blane Griffin and his girlfriend. So it could have been any number of people."

"And would any of those people want him dead?" Anna asked. She felt Jeremy tense beside her, and found that her heart rate had increased.

"I'm not certain Henry was the target. It's possible someone could have meant to kill me. Ellie was always warning me about crazy fans. I did get some letters…" He broke off.

"And?"

"But that's ridiculous." Jeremy leaned up on his arm so that his face blotted out the night sky. "My fans are wonderful people. They happen to love books and love to read. What's wrong with that?''

"I don't see the fanatic fan scenario," Anna agreed. Jeremy was only inches away from her face, and she found it hard to hold on to her train of thought. "Was there anything strange about any of them?"

"There was one writer.... After the fifth or sixth letter, there was a change. The letters became a lot more personal. And the writer would mention that she'd seen me at a store or a movie. It began to be obvious that the letter writer was watching me."

"And that got sort of creepy," Anna finished it for him. "You said 'she.' How do you know it's a woman? Did she sign a name?"

"The letters were always signed 'Your biggest fan.' They were always typewritten. But some of the things—it had to be a woman. Or at least, I hope so."

Anna saw him look away from her as if he were embarrassed. It only heightened her curiosity. "What kind of things?"

"Oh, you know, about my body. Sheer fantasy."

Anna shifted slightly away from him. She was all too aware of his body, and it didn't take a lot of imagination to think of what a woman might write about. Lean legs, cute butt, broad shoulders, capable hands, and that handsome face. Jeremy Masterson was quite a masculine package. He was also capable of mocking himself—another aspect of his character she hadn't anticipated.

"I'm certain you have women falling at your feet," she said, taking care to keep her tone equally light. "Fans and otherwise."

Jeremy's chuckle was appreciative. "Nobody gets one up on you, do they, Anna?"

''Sometimes,'' she said, smiling, too.

''You have a beautiful smile.''

Anna couldn't think of a single thing to say. He was staring down at her, so close that all she had to do was reach out a hand and touch his face. She could see that he was tired and in pain, but he seemed to be ignoring both of those things.

''When we get out of this mess, will you tell me about your grandfather?'' he asked.

Anna felt a surge of warm emotion. For as much trouble as she was in, this was the goal she'd rushed to Kerrville to accomplish. ''I'd like to do that.'' She nodded slightly. ''I think you'll be surprised by what you learn.''

''Surprised and possibly dismayed.'' Jeremy laughed uneasily. ''This isn't going to be pleasant for me, is it?''

Anna reached up and touched his face before she even thought about the gesture. ''Probably not,'' she said.

''What if I listen to you and then do nothing about it?''

Anna kept her hand in place. ''That's up to you. My job was to ask you to listen. I can't be responsible for what you do with the knowledge you get.''

Jeremy brought his own hand up to cover hers. He pressed her palm lightly into his jaw. ''Are you sure about that?''

Anna smiled. ''Positive.''

''Good.'' He eased back down. ''You're an unusual woman, Anna Red Shoes. A little frightening.''

''Why? Because I'm different?''

''That's part of it,'' Jeremy said. ''And because you

challenge a part of me that's maybe gotten a little lazy. Most folks tend to avoid a challenge.''

"We need to sleep," Anna said softly. The intimacy she'd shared with Jeremy was so intense that she was unsettled by it. Whatever challenge she'd thrown at his feet, he'd met and given back in equal measure.

"We need to figure out who killed Henry," Jeremy replied.

"Tomorrow." Anna wanted to stop talking—to stop thinking. She wanted the safety and release of sleep.

"Tomorrow," Jeremy agreed.

FOR A LONG TIME Jeremy lay beside Anna without moving. The fiery pain in his leg had subsided to a slow burn, except when he shifted and set off a three-alarm blaze.

It wasn't his leg that kept him awake, but the woman who lay beside him. He suspected that she, too, was awake, but he knew better than to check.

Sometime during the long evening, he'd accepted Anna's innocence. The thought had crossed his mind that if she were charged with Henry's murder, his own book would help convict her. The idea of that was like a sharp needle in his spine. He wanted to twitch and thrash, but he held still.

The only solution he could see was to figure out who'd killed Henry. He'd gone over the possibilities, but no one he could name seemed capable of such an act.

Irony of ironies, the only person around Kerrville who really had reason to dislike Henry was Blane. Henry had frequently rejected Blane's novels. But only the night before, Blane had dropped the bombshell that his latest work had won Henry's approval.

He replayed the scene at the party. Blane had been drunk. He's also been humiliated by Lucinda's behavior. He might have lied about the book contract to save face. But that didn't give him a reason to kill Henry. Did it?

Jeremy had to go forward on the assumption that he himself had been the intended victim. And his list of enemies numbered well past what could be counted on one hand.

High on that list was Blane. It wasn't only a book competition between them, it was also a woman. And the relationship was further tangled by the long friendship they'd shared. Had they not been such close friends, they could not have become such bitter enemies.

And Lucinda Estar was behind it all. Not that it was her fault. Jeremy knew he'd played as big a role in the mess as she had. But she'd lied to him. He'd had no idea she was Blane's romantic partner, and when he'd found out and asked her about it, she'd told him that Blane had kicked her out.

Just thinking about Lucinda Estar made Jeremy tense up. The pain in his leg was nothing compared to the thought of Lucinda.

She was a real Texas beauty, a woman so stunning that she turned heads wherever she went. Tall, red-headed and built like a goddess, Lucinda knew the potency of her charms and never failed to use them.

Jeremy thought back to his first meeting with Lucinda. It had been at a publishing party in New York. He'd gone solo to the event and he'd seen Lucinda across the crowded room. She'd been standing alone with a glass of champagne, and he'd made it a point to meet her.

That night she had knocked on the door of his room at the Sherry Netherland. It had been one of those evenings with no questions asked or answered. The physical attraction had been strong, and the vast quantities of champagne had done their work. It wasn't until the next morning, when she was lounging in bed and demanding room service, that she mentioned Blane.

Of course, her version was that the affair between them was long over, that Blane had grown tired of her. She'd played the bruised lover to the hilt. And Jeremy had never bothered to ask his old friend. By the time he realized Lucinda was as expert at lying as she was in bed, the damage had been done.

He'd finally broken off the affair in a bitter and ugly scene. Lucinda had accused Jeremy of leading her on with false hopes. He'd roundly denied such a charge. Not a single time had he ever misled Lucinda Estar. He'd never promised her more than what he delivered—a good time while it lasted. That was all he'd ever promised any woman. He wasn't the kind of man who made commitments, even small ones. And he'd been clear about that with Lucinda from the get-go.

Nonetheless, it had been a bad breakup, and now Lucinda was back with Blane. From the hatred he'd seen in Blane's eyes, he could easily imagine what lies Lucinda had told him. The thing that hurt him the most to admit, though, was that Blane could be incredibly hotheaded. Even as a boy, he'd been one to act first and think later. Such as the time he'd punched the high school principal because one of his girlfriends had claimed the man had touched her. Blane discovered, too late, that the girl had lied. It was a pattern with Blane, and one that troubled Jeremy greatly.

He cast about in his mind for other suspects. There was that fan…. The letters had been intense. Toward the end, very sensual. But there had also been the hint of obsession in them. Whoever had written them—and Jeremy was certain it was a woman—had spent an awful lot of her free time following him around. It had rapidly gone from flattering to frightening.

He'd taken the letters to the sheriff, but Lem had almost hooted him out of the office. The story had spread all over town that Jeremy was being chased by a woman and that he'd tucked tail and run.

Even in the cold night Jeremy could feel the heat of embarrassment as he remembered the scene. Blane, in particular, had had a good time with the story. A very twisted version of it had appeared in a New York magazine under Blane's name. Of course, all the names had been changed, but it was clear to everyone who knew Jeremy that he was the target.

After that, Jeremy hadn't told anyone except Henry about the letters. And even Henry had scoffed at the idea that the letter writer might be dangerous. Only Ellie had shown the least concern.

Now Henry was dead.

Jeremy thought through the scene at his home for the hundredth time. If Anna had cut the screen and came through it, that meant the killer had come in the front door. So Henry had either failed to lock it or had actually invited his murderer in.

If he'd invited that person into the house, then it had to be someone Henry knew or someone he hadn't viewed as a threat. Blane would fit that description.

Jeremy sighed and closed his eyes. He needed to sleep. Tomorrow was going to be a long day, and his leg was going to be a very painful problem. Sleep was the best cure he had available at the moment.

Anna had already given herself over to some shut-eye, and to his surprise he felt her turn and press against him. Her arm came across his chest, and she sighed.

Beneath the flannel shirt she wore, Anna was all female. Jeremy was suddenly fully aware of that fact. His innocent invitation to her to sleep beside him was proving to be more than he'd bargained for.

"Great," he said softly. "Just great."

"You okay?" Anna asked softly, still more than half asleep.

"Go back to sleep," he said, and meant it. He tried to resist looking at her, but found that he couldn't. Though it cost him dearly in pain, he shifted and raised up on an elbow. Exhausted, Anna slept soundly on the hard earth.

She was younger, more innocent-looking, as she slept. It was as if she'd given up her hard thoughts and worries and been swept back in time.

Jeremy wanted to touch her. It was an impulse that was definitely sexual, but it was also tender. He reached out and tentatively brushed his fingers on her cheek. To his surprise, she smiled and snuggled closer to him.

The temptation to kiss her was irresistible. He'd been thinking about it—in the back of his mind—all day long. Now he had the opportunity.

He leaned forward to brush his lips across hers—

A rifle shot cracked the night.

Rock splintered beside Anna's head, and Jeremy threw himself over her just before the second shot was fired.

Chapter Eight

Anna struggled against the weight that dropped on top of her. The sound of gunfire was terrifying, but not as upsetting as the feeling of being pinned to the ground, of being suffocated.

"Hold still," Jeremy urged her.

"Get off me."

"Someone's trying to shoot us."

Those words brought her back to reality and she stopped fighting Jeremy, allowing him to drag her closer to the rock that had saved their lives.

"Are you hit?" Jeremy asked.

"No." Anna listened to the silence of the night that now seemed so eerie. "Any idea who's out there?"

"Not really."

She wondered if he was telling the truth. He could be, since the shots had hit close to both of them. Close, but not close enough. They'd been perfect targets in the moonlight.

"How's your leg?" she asked.

"Tolerable," he answered. "Not good enough to make a run for it. I'm not certain if they're trying to hit you or me. Friend or foe. Hard to tell, isn't it?"

"Not likely one of my friends. No one knows where

I am," she answered. It wasn't exactly the truth. She'd told Maria Gonzalez about her proposed trip to Kerrville and her idea to confront the author Jeremy Masterson. Maria had said the idea was nuts and had been worried about it. And Maria had been right. Now Anna was pinned down by gunfire behind a rock with a wounded man. "Any idea how we should handle this?" She was determined not to show that she was afraid.

"*You* could probably ride out of here."

He was stating the obvious, but she was surprised at his answer. He almost sounded as if he appreciated the fact that she'd stayed with him. "I won't ride off and leave you." She wouldn't. For several reasons.

"We can wait them out until sunrise," he said.

"Or I can try to sneak up behind them." This, she knew, was the best—and most dangerous—choice. She could be patient when she had to, but this was not a game in which patience would prove rewarding. Someone out there had a gun and a desire to shoot hot lead very close to them. Waiting around wasn't a smart move.

"No." Jeremy's answer was sharp.

Anna had expected his rejection of her offer, but it still annoyed her. "You're not really in a position to tell me what I can and can't do," she reminded him.

"There could be one person up there—or ten. There could be guards posted all over the place."

What he said was true, but the idea of hiding behind a rock all night held no appeal. "I'll be careful," she said.

"Anna, if it is someone from the posse, what are you going to do?"

It was a good question. She couldn't shoot them.

''I'll just get a look. See how many there are, see how things look. We need more facts before we make a decision on how to handle this.''

''Anna—''

She took off, darting away from the rock and toward the safety of a tree before he could object further.

Anna knew how to move silently over the land. As a child she'd played constantly in the rough landscape of the small town where she'd grown up. And her grandfather had spent a lot of time with her, teaching her the old ways.

She circled the ridge where the mountain lion had been. It was excellent hindsight now, but it would have been wiser to make camp there rather than down by the river. She'd chosen the riverbank camp to allow the horses a place to graze.

As she drew closer to the place from where the shots had been fired, she concentrated fully on her job. The ridge was strangely quiet, as if every single living thing had left it. The sense of being alone was so keen that Anna moved with extra caution.

It wasn't until she'd covered most of the ridge that she accepted the fact she was alone. But someone else had been there. The skin along her back tightened and chill bumps marched over her as she picked up the eagle feather that had been carefully left in a circle of stone. The placement was so obvious that she couldn't miss it, even in the starlight.

In her culture the feather was highly symbolic, but the true meaning depended on who had left it.

Her firm belief was that the rifleman could have killed one or either of them, had he chosen to do so. The shots had been deliberately off. At least for the moment.

And the feather was very much a part of the pattern of the murder. The murder weapon had been a ceremonial knife. Perhaps the person who'd killed Henry Mills *had* actually been attempting to kill Jeremy. It was possible a murderer with deadly intent was trailing them.

And Jeremy was alone, wounded, by the river.

She backtracked quickly, using every caution, to get back to the campsite. It was only when she circled from the river and saw Jeremy, alone, propped against the rock, that she took a deep breath.

"They're gone," she said, slipping back beside him.

"Gone?" He sounded as puzzled as she felt.

"Not a trace of them. Tomorrow, I'll go back up there and see what I can find."

"They're playing with us."

Anna didn't say anything.

"This is a game to someone." He was tense with anger. "A stupid game. Henry's death is all part of some bigger plan."

"I think that's true," Anna answered carefully. "The question is, whose plan?"

"That's what I have to find out."

TIRED, HURTING and aggravated, Jeremy waited for Anna to come down from the ridge. She'd left at first light, and now the sky was pink with morning. Neither of them had slept much. He'd taken the first watch while she tossed and turned, and then she'd finished the night on guard duty while he snatched a few moments of troubled sleep.

Both of them were worn down and edgy.

But his leg, though painful, was not bleeding. That

meant Anna could leave him now and head for safety. He'd be okay until the posse caught up with him and he had a chance to talk to Lem.

He looked up at the ridge and caught the flicker of movement. She had gone back to the ridge to search the area again in the daylight. Now was the perfect time to use the cell phone in his pack. He pulled it out and dialed Ellie's number. She answered on the second ring.

"Jeremy," she said, almost weeping. "I've been worried sick. Let me find some privacy. I'm with the posse. Things are getting worse and worse, and I need to be someplace private."

In the background Jeremy could hear the sound of men and horses. He tried to make out voices, but it was only a blur. Thank goodness Ellie could tell him what was happening.

"Okay," she said. "We can talk now, but only for a minute. If Lem finds out I'm speaking with you, he'll put me in the jail."

"Was Blane in the camp last night?" Jeremy asked.

"Yes…well, as a matter of fact, he wasn't. Not all night. He said he had to ride back for something. He was gone about four hours. Jeremy, you need to come back here and straighten all of this out. There's talk that you might be involved in the murder. Serious talk, not just gossip."

Jeremy fought back his frustration. "Where's the posse located?" Maybe it was time for him to talk face to face with Lem. Ellie sounded truly panicked, and she wasn't the type to stampede easily.

Ellie gave him the landmarks, and Jeremy realized the posse was only a couple of hours behind.

There was one other issue he needed to ask Ellie

about. "Ellie, that knife that Anna had at the book signing. Is it still at your store?"

There was silence. "Why, no. I thought you took it. Lem was asking me about it, and I told him what had happened and that you took the knife."

"You told Lem *I* took it?" He didn't want to press too hard, but it was vital.

"That's right. I left it under the counter. When I went to close up, it was gone. I just assumed you'd taken it as evidence. That's not the knife—" She broke off. "That's the murder weapon, isn't it? No wonder Lem is certain Anna Red Shoes is the murderer. They found an Apache knife at the scene. I never put it together. My Lord."

"I know," Jeremy cautiously conceded.

"Jeremy, this looks bad for you. And for the woman."

"I know that, too. Listen, Ellie, I need to talk to Lem. Alone. Can you arrange something?"

"Jeremy, I have to go. People are coming. If they find out I'm talking to you, they'll arrest me as an accomplice. Call me back—"

The line went dead, and Jeremy felt a surge of frustration. He tapped the phone on the palm of his hand and tried to redial. It was no use. The battery was dead.

He'd lost his connection to Ellie and his ability to influence the posse that was now hunting him. The realization was numbing.

And now he had one more puzzle to solve. Who'd managed to get the knife away from Ellie's store?

That action proved the murder to be not a crime of passion or an accident, but a premeditated act.

Movement on the ridge caught his attention, and he

looked up to see Anna at work. He had to hand it to her—she was one determined woman. And she knew her stuff. If he had to be trapped in the wilderness with someone, he couldn't have asked for a more efficient companion.

Or a more beautiful one.

The night before, he'd come very close to trying to kiss her. Too close for comfort. Now, with daylight flooding the eastern sky, he realized how foolish that would have been for both of them.

She signaled that she was headed back. Jeremy hid the cell phone in his bag. The damn thing was useless now, but Anna would never forgive him if she discovered that he'd had the ability to communicate with the posse. The damnable part was that he'd failed to even tell Ellie he was wounded.

Anna was at his side in fifteen minutes, the casings from two shells in her hand.

"It was someone alone, one horse," she said, looking to the west.

"What kind of tracks? Shod or unshod?" Jeremy asked.

"The ground was too hard." Anna tucked the shell casings into her pocket without meeting his gaze, then turned away. "I'll water the horses."

Making a show out of checking his watch, Jeremy finally looked up at her. "Now's the time for you to make a move. Go on, Anna. The posse could be here in an hour or so. You'd better hit the trail."

Anna looked straight at him. "I can't leave you here wounded. What if the shooter comes back?"

"I'm not exactly an invalid." Jeremy put snap in his voice.

"You're not in a position to protect yourself, either."

She spoke so calmly that Jeremy wanted to shake her. "Anna, you convinced me last night that you're innocent of Henry's murder. But it may not be so easy to convince the others. If you ride on, that'll give me a chance to talk to Lem. I think I can make some headway with this, but it's going to take a little time."

Anna shook her head. "I can't leave you."

"If you stay, they'll arrest you. They're bringing television crews, Anna. Like you said, this is a done deal. It'll be all over the papers. Your name will be ruined. Your professional reputation—think what this will do to you."

She held his gaze. "Think what it would do if the posse rode up here and found your body. I'd be blamed for that, too."

She had him there. He hadn't thought of that. It struck him hard that he'd become a liability to this woman. Never in his life had he ever thought of himself in such a fashion. It was completely humiliating.

Though his leg pulled and burned, he forced himself to his feet and picked up his saddle.

"What are you doing?" she asked.

"Breaking camp."

"We're riding back?"

He walked toward his horse, setting his jaw so that he didn't show the pain. "Nope, we're riding on. If you won't go without me, I'll go with you."

"You can't ride with that leg," Anna said.

He turned to glare at her. "We're both as hard-headed as cypress stumps. You won't go and I won't stay. Saddle up, Anna, and let's go before we're caught here unprepared."

Something in her face softened, and Jeremy thought his heart had stopped. In that split second, he saw how truly beautiful she was when she allowed herself to show a tender emotion. His hand started to move of its own accord, to reach out to her, but there wasn't time. Without another word she began breaking the camp and saddling her horse.

He was ready by the time she'd repacked the equipment and led the two packhorses up. She didn't offer to help as he pulled himself into the saddle, taking as much care as he could with his injured leg. Once seated, it wasn't as bad as he'd feared.

"Is there a ford for the river?" he asked.

"About two miles north." She took the lead and started off at a walk.

Jeremy squeezed his legs around his horse and sent it into a trot. He caught up with Anna and then passed her. "We'd better make some tracks," he said. "They'll be coming hard and fast."

"Jeremy?" Anna caught up with him. "You don't have to do this."

He nodded. "I do," he said. "I started this mess and I'm not one to run away from a fire I ignited. But there's something else, too. There's a chance that the person who shot at us last night is part of the posse."

Anna didn't say anything. He watched her a moment, waiting. Whatever burr was under her saddle, she wasn't going to talk.

Anna nudged her mare a little faster and took the lead. Jeremy fell in behind her. They crossed the river and moved up into land that was even more rugged than what they'd left behind. While Anna chose the path, he kept his attention behind them, searching for any sign of the posse.

There was no calling off the posse—that much he knew. He'd ridden with the same men on two different occasions when they'd been called out to search the rugged terrain for escaped convicts. Once the hunt mentality was in place, there was no keeping it in check. It was a dangerous thing, and he'd started it all with a very cavalier attitude. It made him wonder about the past, exactly how men justified their actions.

Perhaps when there was no justification—just lying.

Anna sat tall in the saddle, moving gracefully with the motion of her horse. She was a remarkable woman, unlike any he'd ever known. Once they were out of this mess, he intended to sit down with her and listen to whatever she had to say.

They reached a small break of cedars where a creek trickled over flat rocks and sand. Anna stopped to let the horses drink, and he moved up beside her.

It was mid-morning and still cool, but Jeremy felt the sweat on his forehead. His leg was throbbing.

"You want to rest for a while?" she asked.

"We'd better keep moving."

Anna looked around suddenly, and Jeremy, too, caught movement behind the trees to the north.

"Stay still," Anna ordered. She dropped the lines on the packhorses and surged forward across the stream—

A rifle shot cracked.

Jeremy ducked as bark flew from a tree beside his head.

"Damn." He lay low on the horse and started after Anna.

"Stay back," she yelled, riding toward the place the gunshot had originated. "Maria!" she called out. "Maria, don't shoot."

Jeremy stopped in his tracks. Two things became clear immediately—Anna knew the gunman, and she had known they were being followed.

"Maria, he's wounded. Don't!" Anna called out.

To Jeremy's amazement, a petite woman stepped out from behind a cottonwood. She wore an old cowboy hat, and the gun she held was a high-powered hunting rifle with an impressive scope. Though she glanced at Anna, she focused her attention on him and very slowly she brought the barrel of the gun up in his direction.

"Hold on, Maria," Anna said, riding in front of the gun.

"You don't know what they're saying about you on television," Maria said, anger clear in her voice. "Half of Texas is trying to track you down."

"It's going to be okay," Anna said calmingly.

"They're saying you're a cold-blooded killer," Maria said. "Orders are to shoot you first and ask questions later."

Jeremy took a deep breath. It was worse than even he'd figured. He held perfectly still.

Anna dismounted and went to the other woman. She put her hand on the barrel of the rifle and pushed it down. "Listen to me, Maria. Jeremy isn't to blame for all of this. Jeremy, come on over and meet my friend, Maria Gonzalez," she called out. "She won't shoot you."

"Don't bet on it," Maria yelled. "After everything you wrote about Thunder Horse…and now you've ruined Anna."

Compared to the cool control that Anna displayed, Maria Gonzalez exhibited the exact opposite. She was hopping mad. And she wore her emotions on her sleeve.

"Maria," Anna said with a warning.

"He deserves to be shot," Maria answered hotly. "I could have got him last night. I should have. Without dragging him along behind you, you could have been to the Mexican border."

"And on the run for the rest of my life," Anna calmly pointed out. Although the situation was still tense, she was relieved to confirm that it was Maria who'd been up on the ridge. The eagle feather had been left to tell her that a friend was at her back. "If Jeremy dies out here of a gunshot wound, I'll be charged with two murders."

"I know that," Maria said angrily. "That's why I didn't kill him. But I thought I'd give you a chance to get away."

"He wasn't holding me prisoner," Anna explained, as Jeremy rode slowly toward them. "He got attacked by a lion. His leg's pretty bad."

"If he dies of infection, then they can't blame you," Maria said. "Leave him."

Jeremy stopped his horse ten feet from Maria Gonzalez. "You're a bloodthirsty little thing," he noted.

He saw the snap of fury in her eyes and realized she was not one for teasing.

"I would gladly cut out your heart," Maria replied with a gaze that left no doubt that she meant what she said. "You have no idea the trouble you've caused. Thunder Horse was a noble man. An honorable man. Yet you wrote whatever you pleased about him. Now look what's happened to Anna, and all because of you."

"Not exactly," Jeremy said, a little tired of the tirade. "A man is dead. Anna was at the scene of the murder—"

Maria spun to look at Anna. "You were?"

Anna nodded. "When I got there Mr. Mills was already dead. I went inside, though. I thought he'd had a heart attack. I didn't know he'd been stabbed."

"With an Apache ceremonial knife," Maria threw in. "So it was your tracks in the blood?"

"I'm afraid so," Anna admitted.

"Holy Mother," Maria said, some of the fire going out of her. "This is a bigger mess than I thought. When I heard the news story, I assumed Masterson had made it all up."

"It's not as simple as that," Anna said. She looked back to make sure the packhorses were still at the small spring. "Maria, we need to keep moving. How far are we from Verde Hill?"

"Half a day—" Maria glared at Jeremy "—if you leave him behind. If we have to wait for him, it'll take longer."

"I can keep up," Jeremy said, angry at the suggestion that he would hold them back.

"We can't leave him." Anna mounted her horse. "And we don't have time to argue. Let me get the other horses. Maria, go ahead with Jeremy."

"I'm not so sure I want to ride off with her," Jeremy said. "She may kill me when your back is turned."

"Hide behind her skirts," Maria taunted. "Write lies and then hide behind the person you've hurt the most. No act of cowardice that you perform would surprise me."

To Jeremy's surprise, Anna laughed out loud.

"Take it easy on him, Maria. He's injured and he's undergoing a conversion."

"What?" Maria asked.

"I'll explain later. Just get moving. I'll catch up."

Jeremy knew Anna was right. Though he didn't like the situation one bit, he actually had no one to blame but himself.

He did have one question for Anna, though. She'd obviously known the night before that the shooter on the ridge was her friend. Why hadn't she said something?

ANNA RETRIEVED THE HORSES and deliberately hung back a little. Though she wasn't exactly surprised to see Maria, she was certainly relieved the feather had come from her friend.

Maria was like that. Once she heard Anna was in trouble, she'd rushed to the rescue.

Anna couldn't suppress a smile at the idea of leaving Jeremy to Maria's tender mercies—trained nursing skills, and verbal flogging. Jeremy deserved it. Once they made it to Verde Hill, Maria's ranch, she could borrow a vehicle and make a dash for the border. She wasn't running away—just getting out of reach of the law until Jeremy could straighten out the mess he'd started. Jeremy would be safe with Maria, and she'd make certain he held up his end of the bargain.

Anna looked back toward Jeremy and Maria. They were arguing. She could easily imagine what Maria was saying. What was surprising was that Jeremy kept his temper. She hadn't expected that of him. There were many things about him she hadn't expected.

The night before, as they'd lain side by side, she'd felt desire for him. Physical desire, yes, but something more. He'd shown her a side of himself that allowed vulnerability. He'd considered that he might have made a mistake. Certainly, he hadn't admitted such, but he had opened the door to the possibility. And when he was wounded, he'd urged her to save herself. There was a hint of nobility in that.

As she caught Maria's voice rising in anger, saying, "I could have hit you if I wanted to, *gringo*," she had to smile. Maria wouldn't see nobility in Jeremy at this point, no matter what he did. Leaving Jeremy at Verde Hill was almost more punishment than he deserved. *Almost,* she thought as her smile broadened to a grin.

With just a little luck, she would soon be in Mexico. Then it would be up to Jeremy to honor his word—to tell the truth about the murder. And about the past.

Perhaps it would all be okay. Once the truth was told, she could come forward and explain what had happened. She had to hang on to that hope—it was the only prayer she had.

She urged the horses forward, galloping to catch up with Maria and Jeremy. If Jeremy could hold up, they needed to make tracks. Maria said Verde Hill was within striking distance. They had to make it fast. That was the only solution. The sooner they got to a phone, the sooner Jeremy could call and tell the truth.

She was still twenty yards away from them when she saw the blood. Jeremy's pants leg was soaked in it, and a small trail of it dribbled from his stirrup and struck the rocky ground.

Chapter Nine

"Leave him," Maria said angrily. "They'll find him. Maybe by the buzzards circling over him." She looked back the way they'd come and shook her head. "The posse is probably an hour behind us. He won't die."

Anna used her knife to split Jeremy's pants leg, though he protested that it was the only pair he had left. "Hush," she said softly. "The wound has reopened. There's more chance of infection." She had insisted that he dismount and stretch out beside the stream where they had fresh water and shade.

"Leave him!" Maria slapped the reins against her palm with a crack so sharp the horse pulled back.

"You're not helping, Maria." Anna's voice was calm but steely.

"I should have shot him."

"You were trying," Jeremy taunted. "You just aren't that good a shot."

"Masterson, if I'd wanted to hit you, there would be a bullet between your eyes," Maria snapped.

"She's telling the truth," Anna said. She examined the wound. It looked clean, but the constant jostling of the ride had reopened it. "Maria can punch a dime that's tossed into the air. Don't doubt her, and don't tempt her.''

"Anna," Jeremy said quietly. "For all of her big mouth, your friend is right. Leave me here. Truly, I'll be fine."

"See," Maria interjected. "He says to go—so go."

Anna swallowed. The sensible thing to do would be to leave him. Maria would stay with him, if necessary. So why couldn't she do it? She remembered her grandfather's warning never to trust the word of a white man. This had to be the reason she was reluctant to leave Jeremy. If she didn't stay by his side, he might recant on his promise to tell the truth. Better to stay with him so that she could make sure he held true to his word.

She looked up from her work to her friend, who was watching her with an expression of concern. "I saw some thistle back by the creek. Maria, would you get some? And some water. We need to build a fire and boil a little of the thistle. I think if we can stop the bleeding, we'll be okay. When we get to the ranch, you can stitch it."

She turned her entire attention to the wound. Since they'd gotten Jeremy off the horse, the bleeding had slowed considerably. He wasn't at risk of dying, but she wasn't sure how much more he could take. Even a big, strong man had his limits.

"You'd risk your life for him?" Maria asked in disgust. "We'll be sitting here playing nursemaid when they catch you."

"The thistle," Anna reminded her. "The sooner I get it, the sooner we can get going again."

"It's a shame you didn't hear the news report before you risked everything. This man did everything but build the gallows to hang you on. That bookstore woman was telling how he'd gone after you to make sure you were brought to justice and didn't escape. It made him sound like Wyatt Earp and Luke Skywalker all rolled into one. May the Force be with you!'' Maria whirled and stalked off down the creek.

''She's one hot-tempered woman,'' Jeremy said.

''We've been friends since we were five. Maria takes it personally when someone hurts me.'' Anna gathered the wood for the fire. ''She talks big, but she's really kindhearted.''

''She'd roast my liver on a spit and eat it for supper,'' Jeremy pointed out.

''No, she wouldn't.'' Anna smiled at him. ''Maria's a vegetarian. Besides, you're far too tough.''

Jeremy's laughter was soft, but Anna heard a note of appreciation in it. The small joke had saved his pride. It was hard for him to be the albatross around her neck. Male ego was a tough taskmaster.

She looked up as Maria returned and thrust a fistful of weeds at her.

''Thank you.'' Anna already had the fire going, and in a matter of moments she'd produced a thin, green tea. She took a cotton shirt from her belongings and soaked it in the tea. ''This should help,'' she said as she put the saturated shirt around the wound.

Jeremy winced and gritted his teeth, but he didn't say a word. Anna looked up to find Maria studying him. She knew what her friend was thinking—at least he wasn't a crybaby. The thistle juice was an astringent and had to burn like hell. Well, at last Maria had found something to like about Jeremy.

''Johnny's at Verde Hill,'' Maria said. ''I can ride on and get him. If you two can make it to the dirt road, about twenty miles ahead, we'll get the camper and meet you there.''

The relief Anna felt at the idea of rescue was offset by the mention of Johnny Severe.

''What's Johnny doing there?'' She tried to sound casual. Long ago, when she'd been young and furious at the treatment her people had received, she'd fallen in love with Johnny Severe. Johnny had worshipped her grandfather. But his take on Thunder Horse was as wrong as Jeremy's. Johnny had seen her grandfather as a man who killed in righteous anger. That was as far from the truth as Jeremy's version of Thunder Horse the Savage. Thunder Horse had killed only to protect the women and children of his tribe. Honor and pride were no reason to kill, and he'd told Johnny that over and over again. It was a lesson that hadn't sunk in for the angry young man. Ultimately, it had been Johnny's anger that had driven Anna away from him.

''Johnny's my partner now,'' Maria said. She didn't meet Anna's gaze. ''He's better at ranching than you might think.''

''I hope so, for your sake,'' Anna said. She felt a stab of anxiety for her friend. Maria had been in love with Johnny for years. Even knowing that his anger left little room for love, she'd longed for him. Anna could only hope that time had mellowed Johnny—and toughened her friend.

''Like I said, I can ride on and get Johnny.''

Maria obviously didn't want to discuss it, and Anna dropped the subject. ''Could you? That's the one thing that might help Jeremy make it to Verde Hill.''

Maria began gathering her things. ''We can get back to the dirt road by eight.''

''We'll be there,'' Anna vowed.

"If he can't make it, leave him." Maria swung into the saddle and took off at a gallop.

"You've got a good friend," Jeremy said softly.

"Yes." Anna began picking up her medical supplies. "And we've got a long, hard ride. The bleeding's stopped for now. I'll re-tie the pressure bandage, and we'll see how you feel."

"I'm ready to ride."

Anna used as much tenderness as she could in pulling the bandage tight, but she knew how much it had to hurt. When she felt Jeremy's hand on hers, she thought he was warning her that he couldn't bear any more. Instead, she looked at him and saw a question in his eyes.

"What?"

"Why *are* you doing this? You've gone way beyond doing the right thing."

Anna didn't look away from him, but she knew she didn't really have an answer. She'd tried to convince herself it was because she didn't trust him. But looking into his blue eyes, she knew that was a hollow sentiment. Her feelings about Jeremy Masterson were tremendously mixed, and she didn't have the time or energy to try to sort them now.

She had to accept that she was doing what she always did—what her gut told her to do. "This is the way I was raised," she said simply. "You don't leave wounded creatures behind."

"No," Jeremy said, "you generally put them out of their misery by killing them. Nature is a harsh taskmistress."

"Killing you isn't an option, Jeremy. Leaving you to die isn't one, either."

His hand tightened on hers.

Anna felt an alarming rush of feelings. His touch was powerful, affecting and so strong that she abruptly stood up. "It's time to ride."

JEREMY THOUGHT THE PAIN would kill him, but he managed to shut it out with thoughts of his next novel. It was perfect. Anna was the female character he'd been searching for. He spun the web of imagination as he rode along beside her, teeth gritted and eyes straight ahead.

At times he felt her glance over at him, and he made sure that his back was straight and his hands were steady on the reins. If he had to die, he'd do it upright in the saddle.

He started putting together scenarios for his new novel. He could see Anna as a figure from the 1860s, right after The War Between the States when the defeated South began to move West looking for a new future, a new dream. Anna was a woman who was strong enough, tough enough, to have survived that era and been successful.

She was also very contemporary. He'd yet to do a modern-day novel.

As the horses moved relentlessly forward, Jeremy retreated from the pain of the ride into his imagination. All he had to do was hang on until they reached Verde Hill and a working telephone. Again he wondered why he hadn't told Anna about his cell phone—now dead—when he was first wounded. Then she could have ridden away and left him, secure that help would arrive.

The question was one he danced around. Sure, he was writer enough to want to see how the episode would play out, but that wasn't why he hadn't called Lem the moment he'd run Anna to ground.

Something else had held him back. Curiosity? Yes, he was curious about Anna. Curious enough to suffer like a crazy man just to ride along beside her. Writing was his life, and she was the germ for a new book, an idea that excited Jeremy in a way that he knew meant it would be an excellent novel. That had to be the reason. It had nothing to do with the tenderness in her eyes, the spirit she'd shown in risking her future for him.

It had nothing to do with the image of her coming out of the river, all wet and sleek and shimmery.

Nothing at all.

He felt a wave of dizziness and grabbed the saddle horn.

"You okay?" Anna asked.

"Never better," he said, giving her a nod.

He was relieved that she didn't press the issue. He was lying, and she knew it.

"I'm working on a new book," he said, because she was watching him a little too intently.

"Yeah."

She was trying to sound uninterested, but he could see the sudden curiosity in her lively brown eyes.

"What do you think about a contemporary setting?"

"You've never done that."

He was pleased beyond measure that she knew that. And surprised at his willingness to talk about his idea. Never, ever did he breathe a word about a book until it was finished. Yet he found himself enjoying the thought of sharing this information with her. And she actually seemed to care.

"What's it about, or can you say?"

He hesitated. "I think it's about a woman who refuses to let life shape her. A woman who insists that she be allowed to shape her own life." It sounded ridiculous, and he chanced a quick look to see her reaction. To his surprise, she was concentrating on what he'd said.

"In my family, we were taught that each person has a destiny. But if a person is strong and true to themselves, they can defy that destiny and pick a new one."

Jeremy felt as if the sun had gone behind a cloud. A chill touched him, and he knew it was because what Anna had said was exactly perfect for his book. She'd given him the theme, the basis for the character and everything that would come after that. She'd handed him a great gift, and didn't even know it.

He was thinking hard when he heard the angry buzz from the sky. Anna heard it, too, and they both stopped their horses and listened.

The look they shared told everything. Neither said a word as they urged their horses into a gallop and headed for the line of trees just ahead of them.

"Damn, Lem," Jeremy said under his breath as he leaned low and gave Jetta her head. They had to make the trees before the helicopter came over the horizon. Once they were spotted, the chase was over.

They reached the edge of the trees just before the chopper swept low on the horizon. Under the cover, they were safe, for the moment. But soon they'd have to abandon the protection and strike out over open land again. The odds on the game had just increased considerably.

Anna turned a strained face to him. "They're pull-

ing out all the stops," she said. "They must think I'm
some kind of desperado. That I've taken you hostage
and that I'm holding you against your will." She tried
to laugh, but it didn't work. "There's really no telling
what they're thinking, is there?"

"No," he answered. He wanted to tell her that the
trouble was even more serious than she knew. But to
do so, he would have to confess that he'd spoken with
someone in the posse. "Let me help you with the
packhorses," he said instead.

She halted, speaking calmly to the horses that were
already spooked by the sudden appearance of the
chopper.

"Look," he said, riding up beside her. The expression on her face was so calm, so steady that he had to
tell her the truth. "I need to tell you something. I—"

The helicopter came straight at them, swooping low.
Tree limbs thrashed and twisted in the wind, and a
fine storm of sand and gravel stung Jeremy's eyes.

The horses began to panic, and he found that all of
his riding skills were required to stay on Jetta, who
was plunging and bucking and trying to run.

Anna was riding the chestnut mare and leading the
Appaloosa and Jeremy's second horse. The backdraft
of wind from the chopper was too much for the packhorses. They reared, terrified of the noise and the wind
and stinging debris.

Anna fought with them for a few minutes, but she
finally dropped the lead lines. She had her hands full
with her own rearing horse.

Jeremy could do nothing to help as he watched the
horses flee through the cedars, carrying all of their
gear.

Using every ounce of his strength, he spurred Jetta

into a dead gallop. He heard Anna behind him, riding like the wind. But no matter how he tried to angle through the trees, he couldn't find a way to head the packhorses off. After fifteen minutes, he pulled up to a walk and then stopped. He was only spooking them more.

Anna stopped beside him. "Let them go," she said. "Johnny and Maria can help me round them up later. They have grass and water. They'll be fine."

He heard the worry in her tone, but knew there was no other solution. They had to keep pushing forward.

"What were you going to tell me?" she asked.

He shook his head. "Nothing, really. Let's ride."

ANNA SAW THE FLASH of the headlights—her old signal—from Maria. Two short bursts of light, then one longer one. The pattern repeated three times in a row. She wasn't one for tears, but she could have wept with relief and hope.

She was so exhausted that she felt as if the last five hours of hard riding had been a dream. Throughout the afternoon, the pursuit helicopter had relentlessly buzzed the rugged terrain, searching for signs of her and Jeremy. It was only Anna's skills that had kept them in the trees at crucial moments. That, and the willingness of the horses to run flat out when they had to traverse the cleared sections. All in all, Anna felt as if she'd been physically abused and psychologically traumatized. The blinking signal lights were the most beautiful sight she'd seen in her entire life.

"Let's ride," she said.

Jeremy, too, must have recognized the flashing lights as a signal and understood that help was at hand. He needed no urging as they galloped together over the last hundred yards of flatland and pulled to a stop beside the camper.

Anna looked in at the dark-haired man behind the wheel. *Johnny Severe.* The last time she'd seen him, he'd been getting on a bus to go to law school. He'd gotten his degree, and now served as legal counsel to several of the tribes. Time had not damaged his good looks nor dimmed the anger in his dark eyes.

"Hi, Johnny. Thanks for coming," she said, wondering what his reaction would be. The last words they'd shared had been bitter, filled with the failure of their relationship and the division of their dreams.

"Where are the other two horses? Maria said there were four."

"They got spooked and took off," Anna said. She glanced at Jeremy, who was taking the scene in with such attention that she felt suddenly exposed. He seemed to be able to sniff out her secrets.

"Well, that's one more thing to take care of."

She heard the anger in his voice and knew that he was furious with the idea of Jeremy Masterson. Maria must have given him an earful.

"They won't be hard to catch. By tomorrow they'll be looking for their groceries." She tried to downplay it, knowing that either Johnny or Maria would have to come back to find the animals. And they would, too.

"There is one small bit of good news." Johnny looked straight at Jeremy.

"What?" Anna asked. The antagonism between the two men was palpable.

"Your friend here is now a suspect in the murder of his editor. It would seem that the current theory among the law officers is that you and Jeremy worked together to kill Henry Mills."

"What?" Anna looked at Jeremy.

"That's right," Johnny said with a hint of glee. "He's the *numero uno* suspect. Anna, you're now an accomplice."

"I presume you heard this on the news. Did they happen to say why I'd want to kill my editor?" Jeremy asked.

Johnny chuckled. "You're a pretty good actor, Masterson. I'll give you that much. I suppose you didn't tell Anna that your latest book was on the verge of being rejected. It seems that Henry Mills found your current work a piece of crap, and had come down from New York personally to tell you all the ways it stank."

Anna could see that Jeremy was dumbfounded. "That's absurd. It doesn't make a bit of sense. Henry loved the book. He was working on the final revisions when he was killed. It was almost ready to go to production. Besides, if they were rejecting the book, they would have sent a letter, not an editor."

"This is where it gets juicy," Johnny said.

Anna could tell that he was truly enjoying himself now.

"The television reporters," he continued, "are saying that Henry had been at your house for several weeks—that he was in the process of rewriting your book for you. It would seem that the publisher has so much money tied up in your career, it couldn't afford to see you flop. So they sent Henry, who did the cleanup, and who you then killed because you were afraid he'd try to take credit for what he'd done."

Anna thought Jeremy was going to fall out of the saddle. She slipped to the ground and went to him, putting a steadying hand on his leg. "Easy," she whispered.

"They said all of that on the news?" Jeremy said, his voice flat.

"They sure did. It was on every channel. And they even had an interview with your publisher in New York, who said he hadn't actually seen the new manuscript, but that Henry had, indeed, gone down to do some work with you. He said you and Mr. Mills had been very, very secretive about the new project."

Jeremy took a deep breath. "This is crazy," he said finally. "None of this makes sense. It's like layers and layers of some crazy plot."

"It'd take a pretty smart man to engineer this scheme," Johnny said, showing his doubt. "It's much easier to believe that you killed your editor."

"And what about Anna?" Jeremy demanded. "Is it easier to believe that she's an accomplice to murder?"

"Nope, I know Anna. She's an innocent bystander. My only question for her is why she's so determined to haul you to safety."

The antagonism between the two men thickened. They bristled like two fighting dogs.

Anna addressed her remarks to Johnny. "We're tired," she said slowly. "We need to get someplace where we can rest." She slid to the ground. "Help Jeremy down, and I'll load the horses."

With that, she led her mare into the waiting horse trailer. She was securing a knot when she heard Johnny's parting shot at Jeremy.

"The news reporters also said the publisher was launching an investigation to see if you'd actually written your last book. It seems that *Blood on the Moon* may have been beyond your literary skills."

Chapter Ten

The voice of the newscaster filled the high-ceilinged den. Comfortably seated on the overstuffed sofa, Jeremy listened to the news reports. Johnny hadn't exaggerated the seriousness. The situation was, if anything, worse than he'd said. Jeremy was keenly aware of Anna, who sat beside him. With each sound bite she seemed to grow paler and more rigid.

Half starved, Jeremy had worked over the plate of fried chicken and hot mashed potatoes that Mona, the cook at Verde Hill, had placed before him. Even as he listened to the news and heard how his literary career was possibly a fake and how he had lied and cheated for everything he'd ever earned, he continued to eat.

Anna was too troubled to eat. Her food sat on the coffee table growing cold. ''I don't believe this,'' she whispered.

Jeremy didn't want to, but he knew it was all too true. It was a surrealistic experience. He felt as if the newscaster were talking about someone who looked like him—his picture was on the screen. A damn good picture, too. Recent. With his mustache trimmed so neat, and a wicked glint in his eyes. It was his latest publicity picture. Looking at it on the television screen as the reporter talked about murder, Jeremy felt as if he were looking at a *doppelgänger* with a bent for evil.

Every single, ugly thing that Johnny Severe had said was being repeated by the newscaster. Jeremy felt the other man's gaze on him, and knew that Johnny was taking a great deal of pleasure in his destruction. There was something else, too. Something in the way he was looking at Anna…

Jeremy's attention was called back to the television. The reporter went on to say that evidence indicated someone was helping Jeremy and Anna in their escape. The celluloid scene shifted to Sheriff Lem standing beside his horse, rifle in hand and badge pinned to his jacket like a cocky Matt Dillon.

The "consequences" to "those people" helping the two fugitives escape would be dire, the sheriff promised, in what was obviously a prepared statement. He drew his brows together and stared balefully into the camera.

Jeremy's leg was the only thing that kept him from jumping to his feet. "Look at that pose! I mean, it's almost scripted out of Hollywood. The sheriff all ready to go out and bring in his man. Lem is an idiot," Jeremy said disgustedly.

"Takes one to know one." Johnny's voice was deliberately pitched to needle. He was casually draped in an easy chair, and watched Jeremy and Anna from a darkened corner of the room.

"Enough," Maria snapped. She leaned forward in her chair. "We can go to prison." Her glare turned to Jeremy. "I do this for my friend, Anna, with no complaint. For you, though, I—"

"He can't help it, Maria. Jeremy's ended up being

as big a loser, or even bigger, than me. He's as innocent as I am. We're both falsely accused," Anna pointed out. "You don't have to like him to understand that."

Jeremy had plenty to say, but he wasn't in a position to say it. Anna's friends were helping him, though grudgingly, out of a tight situation—one he couldn't manage alone. Setting aside the nightmarish accusations now being hurled over his writings, he still hadn't adjusted to the idea that he was a fugitive. He'd thought he understood what Anna felt; now he knew better. To be falsely accused of a heinous act was like having his skin peeled off inch by inch.

His leg was throbbing, but the herbs Anna had put on it had stopped the bleeding. As soon as they'd arrived at the ranch, Anna had examined the wound and found it to be in remarkable condition, considering Jeremy had covered nearly forty miles on horseback. For the moment, there was nothing else to be done for it.

Maria walked in front of him, peering down angrily at him from all of her five-foot four-inch height. "You should turn yourself in, tell the truth and clear Anna," she said. "A *man* would do that."

Jeremy put down his fork. He pursed his lips and nodded, taking a long moment to do so. "You know, that's a good idea," he said, sending a hush over the room. No one had expected him to agree with Maria's statement. Out of the corner of his eye he saw Johnny actually sit up straight. "Where's the phone?"

It was what he should have done the day before— but better late than never. This had gone on long enough.

Maria brought a portable to him without delay and

held it out defiantly. Jeremy took it. He didn't blame Maria for her animosity, but he was getting a little tired of it. Johnny Severe was even worse. He showed his displeasure with a brooding silence and intense scrutiny. Jeremy could feel the man's eyes boring into him now.

Jeremy punched in the number to Ellie's house and waited for an answer. When he heard her soft voice, he felt a wave of relief. "Ellie, it's me. Where's Lem?"

"Jeremy!" Ellie was almost breathless. "Wherever you are, stay there. The whole county has gone mad."

What relief he'd felt disappeared instantly. Ellie wasn't prone to hysterics, but she certainly sounded as if she were about to lose control.

"What's wrong?"

"Everything! Jeremy, you're a wanted man. There's a bounty out for you—your publisher is offering a reward for whomever brings you in. I just heard about it. Oh, it's so terrible. Everybody with a gun is just rushing out to hunt you down like a rabid dog. And they haven't even made the reward public yet. When they do—"

"My *publisher?* Watershed House is offering—" He stopped himself.

"I know. It's almost impossible to believe, isn't it? I just got a call from that young woman you took to the party. Gabriel Wexit. She said she was hanging around up at the courthouse and overheard some of the men talking. It's not official, but I'm afraid it's true."

He felt strangely numb. "How much are they paying?" he asked. Surely this was a nightmare. Publishers didn't offer bounties. This was like some bad episode of "Gunsmoke" or "Cheyenne."

"Two hundred thousand dollars," Ellie said, her voice trembling.

"And they'll get back millions in book sales." Jeremy understood it instantly.

"I've sold six hundred copies of *Blood on the Moon* in the last day," Ellie said, almost wailing. "They're sending a truckload tomorrow. I mean, Jeremy, you're the hottest thing in the book world. You've been on all the networks and cable stations, and even the British tabloids have sent reporters here. They're like wolves." Her voice rose even higher. "They've been interviewing your friends and...Lucinda."

Jeremy groaned. He could only imagine what Lucinda Estar had told them about him. They probably thought he ate babies for breakfast.

"Why did they talk to Lucinda?"

"Because she was willing to talk to them," Ellie said. "And I think they paid her. She said such awful things!"

"Ellie, surely people don't believe—"

"Who can tell what they believe? Some of them think it's all a publicity stunt for your book. They don't believe there's been a murder. Others just want a shot at the two hundred thousand dollars. I mean, that's money that could change a person's life."

Jeremy felt the eyes of everyone in the room on him. Suddenly, he knew that he couldn't afford to tell Maria or Johnny that he had a two-hundred-thousand-dollar bounty on his head. Ellie was right. That was enough money to change a person's life. Verde Hill was a solid ranch, but a large cash infusion would certainly be welcomed. Not to mention the pleasure they'd have in turning him in.

"I need to talk to Lem," Jeremy said into the phone. He kept his tone easy, unconcerned. "Do you know where he is?"

"Out hunting you. You'd think he was some kind of Tombstone marshal the way he's been strutting around."

"Is anyone looking for the real killer?"

"That woman. They're hunting her, but they think you're together."

There was a question in Ellie's voice, and Jeremy answered it. "Whatever else happens, Ellie, you have to make sure that Anna Red Shoes isn't found guilty of Henry's murder."

"What?"

"She's innocent." Jeremy knew Ellie would think over that statement. He didn't have time to fully convince her, but she was a woman who was more than fair. "Trust me on this one, Ellie. She's innocent. If anything happens—just be sure that she's okay. Make sure she has a good lawyer."

"What have you gotten yourself into, Jeremy?"

"Nothing I can't handle."

"Is there anything I can do to help?"

Jeremy was a gambling man, and he was willing to put money on the fact that Lem wasn't sleeping on the hard ground under the stars. It wasn't his style. He might be leading the manhunt, but it was from a motel room with hot water, a phone and a television.

"Lem's not out with the posse, he's holed up in some hotel," Jeremy said. He thought of the places near enough. There was the little motel in Banderos, and a bed-and-breakfast not far from there. He gave

Ellie a quick list and asked her to call and check to see if Lem was registered.

"And if he is?" Ellie asked.

Jeremy hesitated. He didn't want to give out Maria's phone number. It would clearly link her as an accomplice. Even though Jeremy was certain he could sort things out, he didn't want to make trouble for the little spitfire. Not because she didn't deserve a little trouble, but because she was Anna's true and loyal friend.

"I'll call you back in an hour," Jeremy said.

"Tell me this is all a publicity stunt," Ellie begged.

"I wish I could. But since I can't, I'll call you back and see if you've located Lem. Tell him that it's urgent, and that I'll talk only to him."

He put the phone down and looked straight at Maria. "Once I talk to the sheriff, I'll straighten all of this out. None of you will be in trouble."

"Not even Anna?" Maria challenged him.

"Not even Anna," he said, turning to look deep into Anna's serious brown eyes, which watched him so calmly.

Her gaze was like a touch, so physical, so intimate. He needed to talk to her alone, to tell her that the trouble was more serious than he'd dared to imagine. He might not tell Maria and Johnny everything, but he'd decided to come clean with Anna—and to stay that way.

"I need to speak with you," he said softly.

Anna nodded. "I'll ask them to give us a moment."

"No. Why don't we take a walk?"

She looked pointedly at his injury.

"It's okay," he said, and found that his leg was hurting less and less. Anna had the gift of a healer, and Maria had the skills of a nurse. Between the two, his leg had been cleaned, stitched and rebound. "Let's go for a walk."

Jeremy was aware of movement in the corner. He turned to face Johnny.

"Anna doesn't need to be outside with you," Johnny said. "If you have something to say to her, say it here."

"Johnny—" Anna interjected.

Jeremy shook his head at her. "It's okay," he said. "Your friends are only trying to protect you." He wanted to punch Johnny hard in the jaw. But he had to control his temper. He had to keep in mind that as far as Johnny Severe and Maria Gonzalez knew, he might well be a liar and a cheat and a murderer. They had every right to treat him with suspicion.

"No one tells me what to do," Anna said coolly.

Jeremy sensed a hidden message in her words, and when he saw the look that passed between them, he felt the knife blade of jealousy. There *was* something there.

"Let's step outside," Anna said, her touch on his elbow indicating that he should lead the way.

In the kitchen she fell into step beside him, and they exited the house together. Jeremy didn't have to look back to know that a curious Maria was watching them through the window as they left the lights behind and walked into the darkness.

Verde Hill was southwest of Kerrville, on a plateau of good rangeland surrounded by deep ravines and rivers that ran at full tilt during the rainy season but were barely a trickle during the dry. It was country that Jeremy loved, and he took a deep breath.

Anna was at his side, and though they weren't touching, he could too easily imagine how she would feel in his arms. He wanted to touch her. It was ironic that while his mind was spinning with worries and plans, his body was making its own list of demands. Right at the top was touching Anna. Kissing Anna. Feeling the silkiness of her skin, so warm and yet cooled by the night air.

"Your friend has worked hard here," he said by way of opening the conversation. He'd never had difficulty expressing himself, nor talking to women. He'd prided himself on wit and flattery and all of the aids that made him desirable. With Anna, he felt he could not waste her time with such banalities. Yet he couldn't say what he wanted to, couldn't find the words. Anna would be horrified if he turned to her and baldly stated his desire for her—or his jealousy of Johnny.

"Maria's a hard worker, and a good person," Anna said. "She blames you for what's happened, right or wrong. That's the way she is. I'm her friend and you're the enemy. Very black and white."

"Don't apologize for her," he said. "Don't try to explain her to me. I see how much she cares for you, and that puts everything into perspective."

Anna slowed her pace and stopped to look up at the stars. It was a beautiful April night, clear and chill. The lone cry of an owl echoed from somewhere in the darkness. "I wonder how many poets have tried to capture the essence of such a night," she said. "How pitiful words sometimes are."

The rush of desire caught Jeremy so hard and fast that his entire body tightened. She felt the night the same way he did. Was it possible that she was attracted to him, too?

As soon as that thought entered his mind, he pushed

it back. He'd put her in danger. He could be an arrogant fool, but he wasn't reckless. Once they had
cleared up the murder, then he might be free to brush
his fingers over her cheek or to feel the weight of her
dark hair. But not until he'd undone the damage he'd
so carelessly wrought by jumping to a conclusion.

"Anna, I have to tell you something. I want to be
honest."

She turned to face him, and again he felt a rush of
need for her. It was almost overwhelming. He swallowed and started talking. "Ellie told me my publisher
is offering a reward for my capture." He heard her
sharp intake of breath, but she didn't say anything. "I
know you meant to leave me here with Maria and
Johnny. That may be the smartest thing for you, but I
don't think I should stay here. I want to go with you."

"You want to remain on the run with me? Jeremy,
you can stop all of this!" The words rushed out of
her. "Call them. This has gone too far."

"I'm not so certain a call from me will do anything
except send a rush of crazy hunters in this direction.
That's one reason I don't want to stay here. Maria and
Johnny could get in serious trouble."

"They're already in serious trouble."

"Not just legal trouble. Physical danger. I've got a
two-hundred-thousand-dollar bounty on my head now.
Someone could easily get hurt."

"Surely this is some kind of joke."

"That was my first reaction," he said. "If it is, then
the joke is definitely on me. I guess I'm having trouble
believing this myself. I mean, I wonder if they're
printing up posters that say 'Wanted Dead Or Alive.'"

He laughed, but felt the hollowness of his amusement.

"Why would they do this?" Anna asked.

It was a very sensible question. "It's a terrific publicity stunt. Ellie said book sales are skyrocketing. And by tomorrow morning, this will be all over the news." He impulsively reached out and took her hand. "That's why we need to leave now. We can head down to Mexico, just like you planned. Once we're there, it will give me some time to straighten this out."

"You're afraid you'll go to jail?" Her fingers squeezed his slightly.

He heard the amazement in her voice, as if she finally accepted that his role had changed from hunter to hunted. "Yes and no." He wasn't afraid of jail. He was concerned that the justice system he'd believed in all his life had somehow turned against him. He'd learned a valuable lesson. Once a man was charged, the *perception* of guilt was an indelible stain. "I'm afraid *if* I go to jail, by the time all the hoopla dies down, no one will be inclined to actually investigate Henry's murder."

"You want to go to Mexico because of the extradition— You're hoping—"

"I don't intend to hide out. But I'm hoping to buy some time. I've made a mess of it so far, but I can solve Henry's murder myself."

Anna's breathing was shallow and her grip on his fingers tightened. "You don't trust the system."

Jeremy knew their predicament wasn't funny, but he couldn't help a dry chuckle. "Not an inch. This whole thing has escalated out of control. I don't have any faith that Lem can bring it back. I don't know if he wants to." He too clearly remembered the sheriff posing for the television cameras. "Hell, he might get a bid for governor out of this. He's always had political aspirations.''

Anna stepped away from him, finally forcing him to relinquish her hand. ''If you had listened to me to begin with…'' The sentence trailed away in the darkness.

''I never said I was a genius.'' When she didn't say anything, he continued. ''But I do try to be fair, Anna. I know you don't believe that. Whatever my flaws, I try hard to be fair.''

''Your book certainly isn't fair.'' The anger had returned to her voice.

''From where you stand, it may seem that way. All I can tell you is that once we're out of this mess, I'll listen to what you say about Thunder Horse. I gave you my word on that.''

''And if you find you're wrong, what then? An apology? A news conference? You'll have your publisher remove the book from stores? What?''

''Can we wait on that until all the facts are in?''

''Why don't we wait until the next treaty?''

Jeremy heard the bitterness in her voice, and it was as painful as a slap.

''I'm sorry, Anna. For what's happening now. For wrongs that can't be righted.''

''Is this sympathy or pity?'' she asked.

Jeremy knew he was on dangerous ground. Anna could deal with his doubt, his judgment, his rash actions. The one thing she would never accept was his pity. ''I can't change the past, Anna, and neither can you. But I can be sorry for how it played out.''

''Me, too,'' she said, and her voice was hardly more than a sigh. He felt a wave of tenderness so compelling that he slipped his arm around her and held her close.

When she didn't resist, he felt desire surge through him. "As sorry as I am for Henry's death and all of this mess, I have to confess that I wouldn't trade this minute for all the writing awards in the world."

Her smile was luminous in the moonlight. "That's the strangest compliment I've ever received."

"But the most sincere," Jeremy said. His hand stroked her cheek, lifting her face again so that he could look into her dark eyes. "We've shared the magic of the Texas night. That gives us a special bond." He wanted to kiss her. Her eyes were large, liquid. He read the invitation and could wait no longer. He bent his head and lightly brushed his lips across hers.

His hands slipped around her, pulling her close. Anna responded by putting her arms around his neck. He felt her body press against his, and he knew then that her desire matched his.

They'd started out as bitter enemies, but at that moment, Jeremy knew he had never before wanted another woman the way he desired Anna Red Shoes.

Her breathing was ragged as she broke off the kiss. In the chill of the night, her hand closed on his and she tugged him back toward the house.

"I don't want to go back inside," he said. He wanted to kiss her. Again and again.

"Let's go to the barn," she whispered urgently. "We'll find some privacy."

It was all the invitation he needed. He barely restrained a moan of desire as he imagined her, naked, in the hay. But he knew that even his keen imagination wouldn't hold a candle to the reality of Anna in his arms.

Chapter Eleven

Anna awoke with a start. It took a moment for her to realize where she was, to calm herself listening to the steady breathing of the man beside her. She was alert for the noise that had awakened her from solid sleep, but there was only the stamping and snuffling of the horses in their stalls beneath them.

The loft of the barn was dark, but a slice of night sky was clearly visible through the open hay door. In the soft light she studied Jeremy's profile. He was handsome. That pleased her, but there were so many other things about him that touched her heart. He was a wonderful lover, but it was the way he looked at her more than the way he touched her that ignited her passions.

Whatever else happened between them, Anna knew that for one night they had been everything to each other. There had been no room for anything except each other. When she'd planned her trip to Kerrville, this was not the outcome she'd expected. Jeremy Masterson, as a person, had always been a fantasy to her. She remembered something her grandfather had told her—that fate has changed the wind when dreams be-

come solid. Whether knowing the real Jeremy was
good or bad, the experience would change her life.

As she stared at him, Jeremy opened his eyes. A
lazy smile touched the corners of his lips and he
reached for her. "I was afraid I'd dreamed you," he
said.

Anna smiled despite the chill his words sent over
her. "We've been asleep for a while."

The smile slowly faded, replaced by a frown. "I'll
call Ellie and see if she got in touch with Lem. If she
didn't, I'm thinking I should ride back toward the
posse and simply give myself up. I'll get a chance to
get in front of the cameras and tell the truth."

"Sounds good. What if some trigger-happy cowboy
shoots you first?"

"Do you think that's really likely?"

"If I based an answer on how things should be, I'd
say no. Based on what's happened in the last three
days, I'd say I wouldn't be surprised if they've res-
urrected Wyatt Earp and have him on our trail."

Jeremy's chuckle was soft. "You know, I might
have to steal that line of dialogue."

"Be my guest," Anna said, basking in the warmth
that seemed to cocoon them.

Jeremy found his clothes and began dressing. Anna
watched him, aware that he favored his injured leg
only slightly. He was a tough man.

When he was dressed, he picked up her clothes and
offered them to her. Anna took them and stood, shed-
ding the clean horse blanket they'd used as a cover.
The admiration in his eyes as he watched her dress
was better than any words he might have said.

"When this is over," Jeremy finally said, "I want
your word that you'll spend some time with me."

The request took Anna by surprise. "Who knows what will happen when this is over."

"We'll get it straight. Just tell me that you'll give me a chance to get to know you, Anna." He shook his head. "I've never asked another woman to make room for me in her life."

Anna's heart was pounding hard. Whatever she'd dreamed, she'd never expected even a half declaration from Jeremy. "When this is over, we'll spend time together."

"I know you're a woman of your word, and I'm going to hold you to it." He walked toward the ladder that led down to the floor of the barn. "I'll call Ellie and see how the lay of the land is."

"If you can't talk directly to the sheriff, we need to get on the road. I wouldn't change a minute of our time together, but we should get going."

He nodded before he disappeared down the ladder.

Anna slipped on her boots and went down to the horses. Calamity was munching on her hay. The soft sounds of the mare's eating were comforting, and Anna went to the stall and gently rubbed the horse's forehead as she ate.

A tiny scuffling in the feed room sent a chill over her. Rodents. The bane of any barn. She moved down to pat Jetta, freezing when she heard the creak of the feed room door.

"So, instead of seeking revenge for your grandfather, you slept with the man who defamed him?"

The male voice came out of the darkness, and Anna whirled. For a split second she was afraid that one of the posse had somehow caught up with her. Then she grasped the ugly meaning of the words and recognized the athletic man who stepped out of the shadows.

"You have no right to judge me or any of my actions, Johnny," she said coldly. "How long have you been watching us?"

"I'm not a Peeping Tom. I came out looking for you because I was worried. I just got here, but I heard enough to figure it out. I know that what we had between us is over, but to sell out to...*him.* He wrote lies about Thunder Horse. He doesn't care about the truth as long as it fits the old stereotypes. Why him, Anna?"

Anna pressed her palms against her thighs. This was old ground. Johnny, the champion of Native causes, pitted against Anna, the heir of Thunder Horse who refused to take up the mantle of hatred. It was the very issue that had broken them apart when they were college students.

"Your world is red and white, Johnny. Everything is either right or wrong. But life isn't like that. There are all sorts of colors, all degrees of right and wrong. Jeremy made a mistake. I believe he's going to rethink what he's written."

"Ah, the power of love." Sarcasm made his words harsh.

"I don't have time for this." Anna turned to walk away. Johnny's hand on her shoulder was unexpected and painful. He turned her to face him.

"Is he going to retract everything he said about Thunder Horse?" he demanded.

Anna bit her lip. "He didn't say that, exactly."

"Get it in writing. Preferably in blood," Johnny said. "If you don't, he'll go back on his word."

Hanging unspoken between them were the words *"like all the other white men."* Anna stepped back.

At her movement away from him, anger cut across Johnny's handsome features.

"You're beginning to believe him, aren't you?" he demanded. "You'd sell out your heritage for a little…what? Fame? Fortune?"

Anna's first reaction was also anger, but she fought it back. "I don't disbelieve him. He seems to be willing to listen to me. That's a step in the right direction."

Johnny's mouth tightened even more. "Your grandfather would be ashamed of you. After all the lessons, all the talks and the nights we spent listening to Thunder Horse and his bitter experience with people like Jeremy." He shook his head in disgust. "None of it has stuck with you."

This time Anna didn't try to control her temper. "What do you want me to do, Johnny?"

The tight lips curved into a smile. "Turn him in, Anna. Turn him in and collect the bounty. Two hundred thousand dollars would do a lot for you, or for one of those homes for battered women if you wanted to give it away."

"I don't believe you even suggested that." Anna was horrified. She'd never considered that Johnny would contemplate such a thing. Beyond the shock and outrage, Anna had the presence of mind to question his motives. "Why? Why do you care so much what happens to me?"

"I've spent a long time thinking about it, about us." Johnny stepped toward her, and this time Anna held her ground. "If we wanted it, we could have a future. We're the same, whether you see it or not."

The emptiness of his statement made Anna want to

cringe. "What about love or happiness? Is there a place for those things in the future you see?"

Johnny's expression softened. "I'm no good with words, Anna. I'm not a writer, a spinner of lies and fiction. I wouldn't say anything about our future unless I thought we could love and be happy."

Anna felt a flush of shame at her quick words. "I'm sorry, Johnny. I didn't mean to be so... You caught me completely by surprise. What we had between us has been over a long time. You and I both know there's no way to go back."

"I've changed."

Anna realized, once again, she'd taken the wrong tack. The important thing was to get on the road without making Johnny angrier than he was. He was capable of turning Jeremy in for the reward and convincing himself that he'd done an honorable thing. "I don't know what to say," she finally managed to say. "When all of this is over, we'll talk."

He nodded. "I was afraid you were about to ride off into the sunset with Masterson."

Anna schooled her face not to show the emotion she felt. "No one around here is singing 'Happy Trails.' Not for a long, long while. But Jeremy and I are going to have to get this mess settled or we'll both wind up in prison. It's looking more and more like we're going to have to figure out ourselves who killed that poor man."

Johnny put a hand on her shoulder. "Let him take the fall, Anna. No one deserves it more than him. When you told Maria what you planned to do—humiliate him publicly—I thought you were nuts. But then I realized it was perfect." His fingers brushed across her cheek as he leaned closer to her. "As terrible as it is that a man was murdered, you can make it work for you and put Jeremy Masterson out of business forever.''

JEREMY STOWED the last of the supplies in the ranch truck.

"You're presuming that I'll allow you to use the truck," Maria said ungraciously.

"You want me out of here as badly as I want to go," Jeremy pointed out.

"Where's Anna? She's not thinking of going, is she?"

Jeremy held his temper and his tongue. Maria was a loyal friend. He had no right to criticize her, and he didn't have to answer. Johnny and Anna walked out of the barn together and began to cover the distance to the truck.

"She was in love with Johnny all through school." Maria's words were like sharp stones. "Thunder Horse loved him like a grandson."

"Anna's a grown woman, capable of making her own choices, and Johnny is an angry man who's capable of making bad ones."

"You're a fine one to talk," Maria said. She waited until Anna and Johnny arrived at the truck. "They just finished an interview on *Late Edition* with a woman named Lucinda Estar. She had a lot to say about Masterson and his juvenile attitude toward women." She turned to Jeremy. "Seems you're the last of the 'love 'em and leave 'em cowboys.'''

It was the last straw. Ellie had warned him, but somehow he'd hoped to avoid hearing Lucinda's views about him. "Don't believe everything you hear on television. After all, you know what they say about a woman scorned.''

''I taped the show for you,'' Maria said, unable to hide the glee in her voice.

''Thanks. I'm sure it'll be a treasured memory.'' Jeremy checked the ignition on the slim hope the key would be in it. Naturally not. He was going to have to ask for it.

''Along with a fascinating picture of Lucinda Estar's personality and a trauma-filled sketch of her love life, I did learn something interesting....''

Jeremy wasn't certain if it was another of Maria's cat-and-mouse games, but he turned to her, prepared to listen.

''The posse followed the tracks to the road where Johnny picked you up. They also caught the packhorses.'' She answered before Anna could ask. ''They're perfectly fine. They trailed them back to Kerrville.'' She glanced at Jeremy.

He knew instantly what was coming.

''Fancy what they found on your packhorse.''

''What's your point, Maria?'' he demanded, one eye on Anna to watch her reaction. He could only guess how furious she was going to be.

''You could have called help in at any time. You could have had medical attention at any time. You could have stopped this mess before it got out of hand. And you didn't.''

There was no answer to that charge, and he deftly turned the conversation. ''How did Lucinda know that?''

Maria's eyebrows shot up. ''She's riding with the posse. It seems she wanted your hide as bad as everyone else in Texas.''

"It's a total circus." Jeremy held out his hand. "I'm hoping you'll give me the key. I can leave what money I have and my watch, or you can trust me to return the truck or pay for it should anything happen."

"How many times have I heard the word *trust* from lips that were untrustworthy."

"Maria, I don't have time to go through the long list of betrayals and bad treatments that have come your way. I need to move on. The longer I'm here, the more dangerous it is for all of you."

"So this is a noble gesture?"

He was too worn down even to get angry. "Call it noble or cowardly or insane. I don't give a damn how you label it, just give me the damn key."

"Let him have it, Maria," Anna said softly. "Please."

"So Mr. Fiction Writer's heading for Mexico," Maria said. "His girlfriend's been on television giving the world the lowdown on his low-down character." Her smile was like that of a predator.

Jeremy waited for Maria to finish it by telling of the cell phone, but she only shot him a withering look.

"How far is Mexico?" he asked, even though he knew the answer.

"About four hours, but every road is blocked." Maria raised her eyebrows. "Anna knows the back roads, the little dirt paths that no one with a nice car would ever drive."

Anna reached over and took the keys that Maria held in her hand. She gave them to Jeremy, then walked past Maria and Johnny and got into the truck.

"You'd better not let her get hurt," Maria said in a low, dangerous voice as she leaned in the window. "I don't know what game you're playing, or who was sneaking around the ranch last night, but you'd better take care of Anna—or I'll hunt you down.''

''If you want to do something bad to me,'' Jeremy said tiredly, ''you're going to have to get at the back of a very long line.''

ANNA GRIPPED THE WHEEL. It had been a battle for her to make Jeremy relinquish the driver's seat, but his leg had finally made him see reason.

She drove fast but with caution as she negotiated the sharp curves of the dirt road. They were half an hour out of Verde Hill and they both watched the road.

The truck's headlights arced through the black night, illuminating a wall of rock and then a heart-stopping drop down a ravine. This was rough country. She only hoped she'd be able to remember the back roads that would eventually wind them down to the border.

''You're an excellent driver. A woman of many talents,'' Jeremy said. His chuckle made her smile. She shifted her gaze to him, and in that split second, she heard a loud noise and felt the steering wheel jerk in her hand so viciously that it almost pulled her out of her seat.

Anna felt as if the truck had suddenly become possessed by a demon. It lurched forward and to the right. As she struggled to straighten it out, her headlights lost the road. Empty blackness loomed in front of her.

Using all her strength, she fought the wheel to the left and stood on the brake, trying to slow the motion of the careening vehicle.

They were only a few yards from the ravine when she felt Jeremy's body beside her. His strong hands gripped the steering wheel, and he threw all his support into manhandling the vehicle away from the ravine.

At last the truck began to turn away from the yawning darkness. Anna pumped the brake as hard as she could. Slowly the vehicle came under control.

When the truck finally stopped, Anna knew the right front wheel was no longer on the roadway. The truck rocked precariously as they sat there. The headlights illuminated only darkness, and then faded. Jeremy was so close against her that she was pressed into the door. He shifted slightly and the truck rocked, the undercarriage groaning.

"Open the door slowly," Jeremy said in a deadly calm voice. "Open it slowly and move out very slowly."

She did what he said, her body functioning automatically. Her gaze was riveted on the blackness that had almost swallowed them whole.

Inch by inch she moved out of the truck. Jeremy shifted right behind her, so close that their bodies were almost bonded. As soon as she put her foot on the ground, the truck began to shift to the right. In the silence of the night there was only the sound of metal against rock.

"Steady," Jeremy said softly.

His arms came around her and held her still until the truck stabilized again.

"As soon as your weight leaves the truck, it's going over," he said.

Anna had no voice. She couldn't have spoken if her life depended on it. She nodded to show that she understood.

"I want you to push the door all the way open and then dive to the ground all in one movement," Jeremy said. "When you hit the ground, start rolling. Just keep rolling until you feel the bank, okay?"

His breath was on the side of her neck. He held her tightly. Anna nodded again. She knew exactly what had to be done. As risky as it was for her, Jeremy was in an even more dangerous position. Once she got out of the truck, he'd have to get out even more quickly than she had.

"This is going to be tricky, and I'm going to have to jump right on top of you. Roll as fast as you can, but be ready for my weight. And keep your head down."

Anna suddenly felt as if her muscles were paralyzed. Her fingers still gripped the steering wheel.

"Are you ready?" Jeremy asked softly.

She shook her head. She was afraid to speak, afraid that the weight of her words would topple them over the brink.

"It's okay." His hands tightened over hers on the steering wheel. "Let it go, Anna."

She tried to relax her fingers and found that they were permanently shaped to the wheel.

"Come on."

There was a hint of urgency in his voice, and Anna felt his hands soothing hers, massaging. Slowly she flexed her fingers, stretching them out until they were free. She took a deep breath and felt the sweet rush of air into her lungs. She'd been holding her breath for what seemed like a century.

"That's it. Now get ready."

She swallowed. "Maybe we can just ease out together." She was surprised that she sounded so sensible.

"I don't think so. Just push open the door and roll," he said. "And I think we should do this quickly."

"What's the rush?"

"I think someone shot the tire out," Jeremy said. "My concern is that they're out there sighting down on us now. The longer we sit here, the easier a target we make."

Chapter Twelve

This time the fear was a galvanizing force. Anna took a deep breath. "I'm ready," she said.

"Go!"

She pushed open the door and threw herself onto the ground, rolling as hard as she could. Her body registered the rocks that cut into her, but she didn't really feel them. When Jeremy's weight toppled on her, she didn't feel the pain, only the relief that he was free of the truck.

For one agonizing second, the truck seemed to hang on the lip of the road. With another tearing moan, it slowly nosed down the steep ravine.

Anna heard it hit hard, then bounce and hit again. There was a third crash and finally an explosion. She had no time to think about it. Jeremy had pulled her to her feet and was propelling her toward the wall of rock that formed the left bank of the road.

Panting, she pressed herself against the cold stone. Jeremy's body pushed hard against her, compressing her. Protecting her.

"Are you okay?" Jeremy's tone was low and urgent.

"I'm fine," she said, matching his whisper. "How's your leg?"

"It's been better."

They fell silent, listening. If Jeremy was correct—and Anna feared that he was—someone waited in the darkness, watching them. She strained to hear something. There was no sign of any other living creature. It seemed that they were completely alone, but Anna knew that was unlikely.

"Are you sure about the gunshot?" she asked softly, hoping their assailant would believe they'd gone over the cliff in the truck.

"Pretty sure."

Jeremy eased back from her, and she felt the loss of contact—not pain, but the sensation of loss.

"How would anyone know…" She didn't finish the sentence. There were only two people who knew which way they'd gone. Maria and Johnny. "They wouldn't do that. Neither of them." Even as she said it, she didn't completely believe it.

"Let's see if we can't find a safer place to hole up," Jeremy said, deliberately ignoring her statement.

"Okay." She moved away from the rock. Jeremy wasn't wasting his breath arguing about her friends. But there had to be a better explanation. Even if Johnny wanted to turn Jeremy in, he would never, never have risked wrecking the truck and injuring her. Tomorrow, when it was light, she'd find the evidence to support her belief.

"I used to come up here with my grandfather." She didn't mention that Johnny was often with them. "These hills are filled with crevices. If we get lucky, we can find one and wait out the rest of the night."

"It's the best plan I can think of."

There wasn't any point in thinking beyond the safety of the moment. They'd just escaped a fiery death. They had no transportation, no means of contacting anyone. And a killer lurked out in the darkness somewhere.

Anna took the lead since she knew the area. Using the high bank as a shield, they worked their way south. When Anna came to an incline that seemed negotiable, they started up the bank, feet slipping on the shale and loose rock.

There was no opportunity for conversation. Anna concentrated on moving up the incline, on finding a path in the darkness that might lead to safety. All the time, there was the sensation that someone watched her back, waiting for the chance to hurt her.

Behind her, Jeremy's breathing was rapid and hard. She knew the physical strain on his leg was painful.

"Don't think about it," Jeremy said softly. "Just keep going, Anna. If they're watching us, there's nothing we can do."

"Why don't they shoot?" she asked. They were on the face of the incline, painfully exposed. Anyone with a rifle and a scope good enough to shoot out their tire could surely kill them.

"I suspect they want us dead without the inconvenience of explaining a bullet hole."

Anna's foot slid, and it was only Jeremy's hand bracing her that saved her from a nasty fall. "Perhaps your publisher won't pay the reward if we're obviously murdered."

"A brilliant move by Watershed, if that's the case. They escape all liability in making the offer. Yes, a wreck requires no murder investigation and provides the convenience of a body that can't speak for itself."

"So you think it's someone who simply wants the reward money?" She didn't say the names of her friends.

"I wish I could be certain of that," Jeremy said.

Anna let it drop. Her arms were tired from the constant strain of her body weight pulling on them. As a child she'd loved to hike in these hills. She'd loved climbing the bluffs with her grandfather, who never seemed to tire or show physical weakness. With the image of Thunder Horse in her mind, she forced herself to continue upward.

They'd traveled just over a hundred yards when she found a worn area that looked as if animals might have used it as a path. She knew from experience that it could easily lead to shelter. It was the goad she needed to drag herself to her feet.

"Thank goodness," Jeremy said as he followed her up. He, too, stood and looked back down at the way they'd come. "I don't think either of us will need to go to the gym for a while."

It was the perfect remark, a gentle tease of what they'd been through.

"Let's hope whatever animal made this path is smart and on vacation."

"I'll buy the tickets to wherever he or she wants to go."

The path was too narrow to walk abreast, but Jeremy took the lead. Anna was so tired she stumbled, but when Jeremy slowed to check on her, she insisted she was fine. Her grandfather would never have shown fatigue.

They found the opening to what appeared to be a small cave. Jeremy went in first, insisting that Anna wait outside. Without a flashlight or weapon, Anna knew the cave held potential danger.

She listened to the amplified sounds Jeremy made as he moved into the shelter.

"It looks okay," he whispered.

Anna slipped in and immediately bumped into Jeremy. His hands caught her shoulders and steadied her. For one heart-stopping moment, passion sparked between them with the power of a force of nature.

Jeremy held her, his hands strong and comforting as he gently massaged her shoulders. "If I could go back in time, you wouldn't be in this mess," he said.

"If I could go back, neither would you." She no longer blamed Jeremy. Too much had happened for her to be able to focus solely on him. His book, her pride, the unfathomable actions of so many others—it was a circle of blame that had no beginning or end.

"When I was a little girl, my grandfather told me the story of Gray Dog, the son of a mighty chief." Anna's voice seemed to echo strangely in the cave. "Let's sit down, and I'll tell it to you."

"I'd like to hear it," Jeremy said. Together they shifted until they found a wall.

Anna took a seat and felt Jeremy move down beside her. His thigh brushed hers, and she leaned into the contact. His touch was the only comfort in the dank blackness of the cave, and she had no intention of denying it.

"Tell me about Gray Dog."

"He was a rash young man. Because his father was a great chief, he grew up with privileges that many other young boys didn't have." Anna didn't need to close her eyes, but she did. It made it easier to see her grandfather, an old man with long white braids that hung down his chest. His face was furrowed by long hours in the sun, but his voice had been as soft as the deerskin he'd used to make his moccasins.

"Gray Dog was spoiled, but he was also very popular with the other young men and the women. It was said that he was born in a great rain, and that the water from the gods had given him a special charm. He was born laughing, even as the rain pelted down into his face."

"I wish I had a tape recorder," Jeremy said. "I can remember the story, but I'll never be able to recapture the sound of your voice, the way you tell it."

Even though it was obvious flattery, Anna felt a blush of pleasure. "For all of his charm, though, Gray Dog had a reckless streak. It seemed that he had to push the luck the gods had given him. He always chose the roughest horse to break or the longest and hardest journey. For all of the many gifts that had been bestowed on him, he had also been given a blind spot. He could not see the need to let others excel. He didn't understand the importance of stepping back and letting someone else take the honors that came so easily to him."

"Sounds like there may be a moral in this story."

Anna smiled even though she knew he couldn't see it. "Not the one you think."

"Pride goeth before a fall?"

"Keep listening." She leaned back against the wall, relaxing. Her leg was brought fully into contact with his, and a slow warmth invaded her. The cave was damp, and she suddenly shivered.

Jeremy put his arm around her and pulled her against his side. "It's going to be a long time until dawn, and I'm afraid to risk trying to start a fire in here. We'll have to settle for what body warmth we can manage.''

Anna let herself lean against him slowly. He was a solid man, far more comfortable than the stone wall, and he shifted to accommodate her.

''Now go on with the story. I hate it when I can't guess the ending.''

Anna's laughter echoed softly in the cave. ''Gray Dog fell in love with a young woman, a beautiful girl whose mother had been taken in a raid.''

''She was white,'' Jeremy guessed.

''Yes, the mother was. Therefore the girl was not a proper wife for the son of the chief. All of his skills and talents could do nothing to change the facts of her birth.''

''But he married her anyway, right?''

Anna punched him lightly. ''If you'll let me finish without interruption, the story would go much faster.''

''Sorry,'' he said. ''I keep trying to write the script.''

''He married the girl that was chosen for him, not the girl he loved. He'd become so used to having the approval and love of his people that he couldn't step outside of it, not even for the woman he loved.''

''And what became of the girl he loved?''

Anna smiled, wishing she could see his face. ''She became the mother of Thunder Horse.''

Jeremy's exhaled. ''Is this true?''

''According to my grandfather. Gray Dog was like an uncle to him. It was sad, because Gray Dog never had children. But he did tell my grandfather many things. I was thinking about one of them as we were climbing up to the cave.''

''And that would be?''

"Never lay blame. For a long time, Gray Dog blamed his wife because he couldn't marry the woman he loved. It was for that reason that the gods never gave them a child."

"He blamed his wife for his own weakness?"

"That's often the path of blame. But he eventually learned, and he told my grandfather the lesson—wherever you try to leave blame, some gets on your shoes and you track it back home."

Jeremy was quiet for a long time. "Sometimes blame has to be placed. Whoever killed Henry has to pay. Whoever is out there trying to kill us deserves to be punished."

"This whole mess started when I went to that bookstore with the idea of making you pay for what you'd written." Anna shifted so that she was looking at him, even if she couldn't see. Now the blackness was like a shield; she could speak truthfully. "I think that's the kind of blame Gray Dog was talking about. I blamed you for the past because you'd written about it in a way that brought back all of my grandfather's suffering."

Jeremy reached out into the darkness. His fingers brushed lightly across her face, feeling her cheeks and then tracing down her jaw so gently that it was like a whisper. "I want to know more about your grandfather. I want to know everything."

Anna nodded. "I'll tell you whatever you want to know."

"Because you want me to correct the image of him I painted?"

"Because you should have known him, Jeremy. He was a great man. A wise man."

"He taught you a lot. I can see that. Wise and beautiful."

His fingers moved down her neck, a featherlight touch that only made her want more. Anna's heartbeat increased at the boldness of what she was about to do. "I may not be wise, but I'm smart enough to ask you to kiss me." Her body tightened in anticipation.

"Are you sure?"

She couldn't tell if Jeremy was gently teasing her or truly hesitant. "No, but we may not get out of this cave alive. With so much on the line, the risk of one more kiss seems reasonable."

Jeremy chuckled softly as he leaned to brush his lips across hers. Anna liked the feel of his soft mustache. She held back and let him come to her. The first tentative sweep of his lips became a deeper kiss.

His arms slipped around her, and he pulled her into his chest. He deepened the kiss, and Anna found her desire for him growing fast.

Jeremy's eased back, his voice rougher than usual. "I could tell you that I've never wanted a woman the way I want you, but I suspect you'd laugh at me."

Anna did, a gentle rejoinder to his teasing. "I wouldn't laugh, I'd just say that you'd had a lot of practice seducing women."

"No point denying the past," Jeremy said. "But the terrible truth is that I mean it. Anna, I've never met anyone like you. From the first minute I saw you in the bookstore, I was attracted. Your anger was so…passionate. I wanted you, and I wanted to shake you until you saw reason. I've never had a woman affect me in such opposite ways."

"My grandfather said I could infuriate while also eliciting awe. He didn't mean that as a compliment."

She shook her head. "He loved me a lot, so he was willing to put up with the infuriating part."

"I want to kiss you again." Jeremy's hand traced slightly lower, his palm grazing the top of her breast. "But that's not all I want."

"For a man who's been clawed, forced to straddle a horse over some rough terrain, shot at and made to climb a cliff, you talk mighty big." Anna could feel her heart pounding. She wanted him again. One taste had only whetted her appetite.

Where her passions would take her, she could only guess, and heartbreak seemed a likely destination. He had his world and she had hers, and they were far, far apart. Putting an end to this banter was the smartest thing to do. *Now.* But she found that she couldn't.

"I should be in the grave, or at least in a hospital bed, but you excite me, Anna. I want to touch you, to kiss you, to make love to you. Even on this stony floor. I don't care where."

His words pulled at her, fanning the flame of her own desire. She thought of the danger outside, and the passions inside that were growing with each passing second.

"Kiss me," she said.

He pulled her into his lap and tilted her head back so that he could kiss her deep and long.

Anna felt as if imaginary restraints throughout her entire body were snapping and falling away. Jeremy's kiss was like the first time. She felt as if she'd never experienced a man's lips on her, never felt the passion aroused by the intimacy of his tongue.

Her skin was hypersensitive, and her blood pulsed. As she reached her arms around his neck to hold him more tightly, curling her fingers lightly in his hair to hold on, she knew that whatever else happened, she was, at that instant, changing her life forever.

THE FEEL OF ANNA in his arms was like magic. He wanted her so desperately, and yet he had never felt such tenderness for a woman. The pain in his leg completely disappeared, and he forgot he was on the hard floor of a cave with someone outside trying to kill him.

There was only Anna, the feel of her, the smell of her hair, the way the tiniest of his touches brought a response from her that made him feel as if he would die without release.

Beneath the physical sensation was another level of awareness. Jeremy knew he'd always been a man who felt that he could forge his own destiny. Hard work, discipline, focus—those were the tools at his disposal to carve out his life. He was the man, the one who spotted the woman and then went after her. It was his timetable that determined the course of events.

None of that was true with Anna. He wanted her without regard for any of his own rules. He wanted her despite them—knowing that she would disrupt all of his carefully laid plans.

It was the most joyous experience he'd ever known, and he wanted to savor every second of it. He reined in his need and very slowly began to unbutton her cotton blouse. She trembled in his arms, and the thrill of it was almost more than he could stand.

His hand moved over the flat of her stomach—skin so soft and warm that he nearly lost his unstated desire to go slowly. As his fingers moved up to touch the swell of her breast, the sound of a rock sliding outside the cave halted him.

Anna, too, froze. Together, in the darkness, they held their breath and listened.

It had been the tiniest of sounds, something a small animal could make. Or it could be the sound of a deadly predator moving ever closer to them.

Anna sat up, and he eased her over to the floor of the cave. His hand on her shoulder cautioned her from moving. In his own head, he could hear his breathing, harsh and shallow. But he knew he wasn't making a sound. Nor was Anna. They simply waited and listened.

When he was almost ready to give it up, he heard the slip of another fragment of shale. The rock tumbled down the incline they'd just climbed.

Whatever was out there was on the path that led to the cave.

Whatever was out there had slipped, and there was a scrambling noise as it tried to regain its footing.

"Human," Anna said in a whisper that was more air than sound.

"Are you certain?" For all of his skills, he knew Anna was a superior wilderness person. She'd had the best of teachers and an inborn skill that his years of practice could never rival.

"Human," she said again. "Maybe two of them."

Jeremy knew what he was going to do would anger Anna, but there was no choice. He was sick of being hunted like some wild animal. He was afraid that somehow Anna would be injured. His hands tightened on her shoulders.

"I'm going out there and put an end to this," he said. He rose as he talked, his hands pressing her to the ground.

"Don't be a fool," she whispered. "Whoever it is

seems to want you dead, probably more than they want me dead.''

''Exactly,'' he said. ''It's me they're after. If I turn myself over to them, you'll have a chance to get out of this.''

''Think, Jeremy!'' Anna grabbed his arms, her fingers digging in with the intensity of her words. ''You walk out there, and they'll kill you. Dead men don't carry tales. We've already figured this much out.''

Her argument was persuasive, but even more wonderful was her passion. Jeremy swallowed. She cared what happened to him. Even after all that he'd done, she was still willing to risk herself to help him.

And that was the one thing he couldn't allow to continue. He stepped back from her, pulling free, and headed out the opening of the cave.

Chapter Thirteen

Jeremy stepped into the night, half expecting to feel a bullet tear into his flesh. His hand went instinctively to his side, where his gun should have been. The weapon Maria had loaned him, like everything else, had gone over the side of the ravine with the truck.

When he was only five feet outside the cave opening, he tensed and listened. Far in the distance a coyote howled a lonely complaint. Nearby there was only an eerie silence.

Yet someone *had* been outside the cave.

Where had they gone, and what were they intending?

Those questions would be answered only by figuring out who had killed Henry. Sadness and anger that he'd rigidly held at bay swept over him. His friend was dead. He hadn't wanted to consider what it might be like to work without Henry—what the loss of that friendship might mean. Up to this moment, he'd managed to keep his gaze focused not on the loss of a friend, but on revenge. And, he silently vowed, whoever had killed Henry *would* pay.

The night was still dark, and he studied the sky to get his bearings. The Big Dipper was a wanderer's friend, and he traced the pattern, firmly establishing his location. He didn't want to get lost and not be able to find Anna. He would return to her as soon as he was certain he wasn't bringing danger back with him.

He set off at a slow, careful pace. When his foot brushed the rock, he wasn't certain what the familiar noise was, but he halted. There had been a flutter. He thought of the soft and deadly rattles of some of the big snakes that loved the rocky terrain. But it was too early in the year, the nights too chill. The cold-blooded reptiles hadn't yet come out for the summer.

He shifted his foot, pushing the stone around. Again the sound. He knew it this time. Paper. Bending down, he found a sheet of paper had been placed beneath a rock. The deliberateness of the setup was clear to him. Someone had climbed up the side of the steep hill to leave this for Anna or him.

He picked up the paper and held it, uncertain what to do. Someone had chosen to leave a message rather than move in for the kill. *For the moment,* his mind added. This was like some kind of sick game, he thought again.

He knew he needed light to be able to read the note. But it could also be a ploy, an attempt to get him to light a fire so that he'd then be a perfect target for a shooter who'd crept close and was watching from the safety of the rocks.

There was really only one thing to do. Go back inside the cave, use the cigarette lighter he carried, and read the message.

He was about to do just that when he felt a light brush against his back. *Anna.* It was an interesting discovery to find that he'd been half expecting her.

''I don't suppose it would do any good to order you

back to safety.'' Since he didn't know from which direction danger could come, he couldn't even try to shield her.

"I know you're a skilled tracker, but a man can get lost up here in these hills."

Anna's voice held a bit of teasing, but also something deeper. Jeremy felt his pulse begin to race. She'd been worried for him.

"I didn't make it far enough to get lost." He put the paper in her hand, fumbling slightly in the process. "We have a message."

"Let's read it." Paper in hand, Anna started moving to the cave.

Jeremy followed her, and, when they were inside, pulled the lighter from his pocket. He held it a moment, knowing that in the darkness she couldn't see him.

"You have such a strong connection to your family," he said as he found her hands and put the lighter in them. "I have a few stories. A lot of tales sprang up about my grandfather."

"The famous Bat Masterson."

It pleased Jeremy that she knew. It had been on the dust jacket copy of some of his books.

"A lot of that stuff was Hollywood fabrication. Folks tended to think the television series was created from fact. Even this cigarette lighter was purported to be his own personal relic. It's a Zippo." He laughed. "It's hard to believe people are so gullible, so easily led…" He held the lighter in her hand and stopped. "Which is exactly what you've been trying to tell me."

"Light the fire," she said, pressing it back into his hand.

"No." He reached out into the darkness of the cave and caught her hand. She was letting him off the hook without even taking a moment to enjoy watching him wriggle. "I'm about as hardheaded as this rock, but I finally do understand."

"Light the fire," Anna insisted. "We can hash out our personal problems after we figure out how to survive this latest twist of fate."

"Okay," he said, flicking the wheel of the lighter. A yellow flame illuminated Anna's face, and he thought how he'd love to see her by candlelight. She held the paper he'd given her. Anna moved close to him and held the page at the ready.

At first glance, Jeremy found that his eyes refused to focus on the page. It was typewritten text. Then he recognized it—instantly. It was from his next novel, the sequel to *Blood on the Moon*. It had come from the stack of manuscript pages on his desk at home.

The page had been taken from the fourth chapter and dealt with his hero's breakup with a grasping socialite who wanted to turn the cowboy into her drawing room "pet." He'd been particularly proud of the scene because he thought he'd shown Hank Chisholm's desire to be fair and tender toward Lorraine Ellison.

The storyline came rushing back. In the first book, Hank had been smitten by Lorraine's beauty and charms. He'd even been attracted by her polished manner and the ease with which she moved through society. But as he grew to know Lorraine, Hank had become more and more aware of her manipulations, her true unhappiness—except when controlling Hank.

"Jeremy?"

Anna's voice called him back from his thoughts. He felt a hand on his arm.

"What does it mean?" she prodded.

He looked down at the page. "It's from my book. It's what Henry was editing when he was killed."

The tiny fire dimmed and then flickered back up. In the dancing light he saw that Anna was staring at him as if she were trying to interpret a complex puzzle.

"I'm not sure I appreciate the significance," she said.

Jeremy was certain that he did. "In the book, my protagonist, Hank Chisholm, is breaking up with the woman he thought he loved."

"Oh, yeah, the greedy and manipulative Lorraine," Anna said eagerly. "I hated her in the first book."

Jeremy was truly stunned. "You knew she was like that? From *Blood on the Moon*?"

"From the first minute she stepped onto the page," Anna said.

"But Hank didn't." He felt compelled to defend his character.

"Men seldom do, until it's too late." Anna chuckled. "You should read some books written by women, Jeremy. We read your books and learn a lot of things about how men think. It might prove to be helpful if you took the time to do the same."

"Literary criticism aside, I think this page is a real clue," Jeremy said. He had no real proof. Just a hunch. But in his heart he felt as if he'd stumbled on the truth. As blind as Hank, Jeremy finally saw the parallel.

"What kind of clue?"

"I broke up with a woman who was something like Lorraine. I didn't realize it at the time, of course. This scene is a reflection of what was happening in my real life.'' The light flickered and went out.

"This woman…'' Anna hesitated.

Jeremy couldn't see her in the darkness; he could only hear her. He waited.

"Are you saying that the woman who represents Lorraine in your books might have something to do with the murder?''

He took a deep breath. "I know it sounds crazy. You probably think my ego has squeezed the life out of my brain. But this page—this particular page—is where Hank realizes how truly dangerous Lorraine is, and he decides to tell her he's moving on. But she won't let him. She threatens revenge and vows that he'll regret the day he ever met her.''

For a moment there was only silence. The tiny fire burned down to a glowing ember, then went out.

"Let me ask a question,'' Anna said. "Does this reflect the truth of how you broke up with your friend?''

Jeremy cleared his throat. "I thought I was doing a really good job of being careful with her, of trying to make it seem that I was the one at fault, that there was something wrong with me that had nothing to do with her. But she wasn't having any of that. She told me bluntly that she would make me pay for 'leading her on.'''

"This is Lucinda Estar, isn't it?''

Jeremy nodded, and when he realized she couldn't see, he admitted it was true.

"Listen, I think you've got yourself in a real mess here,'' Anna said carefully. "If your hunch is correct, that woman is right outside this cave, and she means to kill you. And probably me, too.''

Jeremy wanted to deny Anna's conclusion. It was ludicrous. He'd broken up with women before—dozens of them. And none with the caution and finesse he'd used on Lucinda Estar. But then he remembered the recent party she'd crashed, provoking quite a scene. It was a galling situation for Blane. Everyone in the room had been whispering that Lucinda only went back to him because Jeremy had dumped her.

"Maybe you should yell out the cave that you're willing to marry her," Anna suggested.

Jeremy felt her humor like another arrow in his heart. "Very funny. But to be honest, I think I'd rather take my chances."

"That bad, huh?"

He heard the hint of relief in Anna's voice and he felt a flood of desire for her. She might tease him, but she didn't want him with another woman. Not even if it meant sacrificing her safety.

"It wasn't bad while it was happening. It's only looking back that I realize how bad it was. Lucinda can be very compelling. She's also extremely attentive and socially facile. She gave me a view of a world I thought I wanted."

"Thought?"

"Once I was in it, I realized that my heart was in the hills. I want to live on my ranch and write. I want to be able to saddle up and ride out and bring in the cattle or check the fence line. All of that fancy living looked good, but it wasn't right for me."

"Or her?"

"Ranch life is the last thing she wanted." Jeremy flicked the lighter again, catching another quick glimpse of Anna's face. "No matter what she says, it's long been over."

"How did this Lucinda figure out where we were and where we were going?" Anna asked.

"That's a very good question." Jeremy didn't have an answer for it, either. "She was riding with the posse, according to the news reports."

"Johnny may have told her our route."

Jeremy felt a tingle of jealousy. "I can see where he might want to get rid of me, but to put you in danger?"

"I don't think he would have known she was trying to kill you, or us. And he'd want to believe that she was in love with you."

Jeremy couldn't argue that point. He knew firsthand how convincing Lucinda could be. If she presented herself as the girlfriend, it would give Johnny a double reason to want to help her. There was something else troubling him, though. "How did Lucinda get this page of manuscript? There was one copy, and it was beside the computer in the room where Henry was killed."

Anna was silent. "You told me earlier that she was at a party, drunk and angry. Is it possible she was so drunk that she went to your home and accidentally killed Henry thinking he was you?"

Jeremy didn't have an answer. "When she's angry, she's completely irrational. And she was drinking. But to stab a man several times…I don't know." He reached in the darkness and found her hand. "Anna, I think we should sneak out of here before daylight."

"Traveling this terrain at night can be treacherous."

"Staying here can be worse. She knows where we are. We have to put enough distance between us that we stand a chance." It wasn't a good solution, but it was the only one he could think of.

"Okay," she agreed. "Be sure and take that page. It's the only evidence we have."

Jeremy struck the lighter again and looked at the page. He heard Anna's sharp intake of breath.

"There's something on the back."

He turned it over. The handwriting was bold. "'Tell the publisher that I won't sign unless the advance is more than Jeremy's'," he read aloud. Jeremy held the page for a moment, folded it and put it in his pocket.

"What does it mean?" Anna asked.

"It means Blane was in my house, talking with Henry the night Henry was killed," Jeremy said slowly. "It looks like the notes from a contract negotiation that might have gone wrong. Let's get moving. Lucinda may not be alone, and Blane's as good with a rifle as I am."

ANNA STUMBLED across rocks, thistles and a thousand other unidentifiable objects that seemed determined to flail the skin from her face and hands. She was exhausted when she and Jeremy found themselves, at dawn, back on the road—exhausted, elated and afraid. They could walk toward freedom on a reasonably level roadbed. But they were also right in the path of anyone who came looking for them.

"I think we need to take a break," Jeremy said.

She took one look at him and knew that as tired as she was, he was in worse shape. He'd had to favor an injured leg. Anna was also troubled by the conclusions Jeremy had come to. The page from the manuscript was damning. But why would Lucinda or Blane go to all the trouble of planting the page without killing them? And why leave the page at all? If they'd been close enough to leave the message, they could have put the barrel of the gun in the mouth of the cave and finished them off.

"This looks like a good place." Jeremy pointed to a cluster of rocks off the road.

Anna nodded agreement. If they scrambled over the outer ring of stones, they'd be completely concealed. Yet they'd be able to hear any vehicles headed their way. She and Jeremy both were hoping that a ride would come along. It was probably a futile hope, but it was all they had to cling to.

She made sure Jeremy was comfortably settled. They were both desperate for water, though neither of them had said a word about it. She checked the sun. The night chill was burning off fast, and by noon it was going to be blazing hot. How long could they go without water?

"Any chance Maria might come looking for you?" Jeremy asked.

Anna had considered the possibility. She was certain Maria wasn't involved in anything that might have harmed her. "Maybe, if she has any idea that we aren't already in Mexico." She didn't want to build false hopes—for either of them.

"I think you should strike out on your own. You can travel faster without me. And if it really is Lucinda or Blane, maybe they'll stick to tormenting me, and leave you alone."

"Maybe," Anna said again.

"You're not very conversational this morning."

She saw that despite his fatigue and pain, he hadn't lost his sense of humor. "I'm not leaving you. With my luck a coyote would find you, drag you off, and I'd be stuck with the title of murderess. You forget, you're the only person in this mess that can help me prove my innocence.''

"This is perfect justice. I'm now the albatross of truth in your life."

Anna couldn't help but smile. "It is a strange twist of fate."

"Do you have any idea how far we might be from civilization?"

Anna had been trying to calculate. She'd once known this land well, but it had been years since she'd traveled through it. "There was an old homestead not too far from here. Who knows if there's still anyone there—but at least there may be water."

"Can you find it?"

"May—"

"Don't even say it."

"I'm pretty sure."

"Then I'm asking you to go on without me."

Anna studied him. Was he tired or trying to be noble? It was impossible to tell. He was right. She could make a lot better time without him. And he was as safe as he could be in the seclusion of the rocks.

"I'll be here when you get back. Bring some water, and a vehicle or horse or mule…or wheelbarrow."

Anna got up and went to him. Kneeling beside him, she checked his leg. There was a trace of fresh blood, and the leg was swollen and hot to her touch. Classic signs of infection. It had been healing perfectly, but all the trauma of leaping from the truck and climbing had irritated the wound. Walking would be the worst thing he could do.

"Okay," she said, "but stay here. Don't leave for any reason. I'll be back as quickly as I can." Her inclination was to stay with him, but there was little else she could do. He was going to have to have medical attention, and soon. She had to go.

"Be careful," he said. He reached up and grasped her hand, pulling her gently toward him.

Anna responded to the kiss with a passion that hit her hard, but she forced herself away. She had to leave while the air was still cool. She wasn't injured, but her own reserves had been taxed by the sequence of events.

"Go," Jeremy said softly. "I'll be waiting for you."

HE WATCHED HER CLIMB over the rocks, and felt relief. Ever since they'd stopped in the rocks he'd had the sense that someone was watching them. Perhaps it was only his imagination, or his fatigue playing tricks on him.

Perhaps it was real. He wanted Anna gone.

The manuscript page had troubled him far more than he'd let on. He'd assumed that Henry's murder had been accidental—that *he* was the target. But the page proved that the murderer was either incredibly calculating or so devious that he or she could turn any mistake to her advantage.

That page had to have been taken during the murder, *or by someone investigating*. Who else would have had access to his home?

The sun inched up in the sky, and he felt the sweat appear on his forehead. It wouldn't be long before he'd be too hot. With each passing hour, his need for water would become greater and greater. He'd written this scene in *Blood on the Moon*. He knew the end result, and it wasn't pretty.

To take his mind off his pain and thirst, he mentally

compiled a list of suspects. Lucinda and Blane were first and foremost, either together from the beginning or falling in cahoots due to circumstances.

Jeremy thought about his former friend. He and Blane had once been inseparable. They'd learned to shoot and ride and herd cattle together. They'd studied the skills of tracking and the ways of the old West, first for pleasure and then for research for their books. Blane was a highly intelligent man. And he was a very jealous man. From his studies of human nature, Jeremy knew that jealousy was one of the key motivators for murder. Blane was jealous and he'd been humiliated. Jeremy considered him a serious candidate.

He also considered both Maria Gonzalez and Johnny Severe as possible suspects. Maria was highly volatile. In truth, though, she lacked a real motive— other than revenge for what he'd written. And Henry would not have been the target. Johnny was a wild card. Jeremy didn't doubt his involvement in the most recent turn of events. But it was a stretch to believe that the angry man had plotted the murder of Henry Mills. All because of a book.

Surely his words hadn't incited anyone to violence.

He knew better, though. Recent court cases involving writers and filmmakers who were being held accountable for the actions of their audiences were all over the news. Unstable people could be prodded over the edge with the least little thing.

Even a book.

But surely the killer had realized, at such close range, that Henry was an innocent bystander. Yet he— or she—had killed him. And in a violent way. Because he struggled? Because he knew his attacker? Because he frightened them? Because— Jeremy closed his eyes and fought against the wave of frustration. He was tired and his leg throbbed with a knife-like edge of pain.

The sound of something scuttling in the rocks close by made his eyes snap open. He craned his neck, expecting to see that Anna had changed her mind and come back. Instead, what he saw forced him to draw in a sharp breath.

"Get up," Johnny Severe said, pointing the gun at him.

"What do you want?" Jeremy said. He didn't know how to play this scene.

"Get up and come with me. I'm not going to tell you a third time."

Jeremy rose slowly to his feet. The pistol was a Colt .44, and Johnny looked as if he knew exactly how to use it.

"Where's Anna?" Johnny asked.

"She went to look for water."

"The old Rivers's place. I was wondering if she'd remember. But she's like her grandfather—she never forgets a thing."

Jeremy didn't think there was admiration in Johnny's tone. "What are you planning to do?"

"Well, the way I see it, I've got a couple of choices. I can make you disappear and see what happens, or I can turn you in for the bounty your publisher is offering. Now that seems like the wise choice. Verde Hill is doing okay, but a little capital infusion could make all the difference in the world."

Jeremy knew it was futile to argue. "What about Anna?"

"What about her? I waited until she was clear of this. Once I turn you in, I'll come back and get her.

She's okay. She could last out here for a week if she wasn't saddled with you. And she won't be." He waggled the gun barrel. "Let's get moving."

"And Maria?"

"My soon-to-be ex-partner? She's at the ranch." He laughed. "I told her I had to go into town to talk to the accountant about taxes."

"You could have killed Anna when you shot out that tire." Jeremy decided to try an assault. "What kind of creep are you?"

Johnny's eyebrows arched. "You're mighty free with assigning guilt to other people. But that's not really a concern right now. The only issue at hand is whether you're coming with me willingly or whether I'm going to have to resort to what you call in your books 'physical violence.' Don't give me a chance to pick out what I'd prefer. You won't like it. I can promise you that."

Jeremy felt panic rising, not for his own safety but at the idea of leaving Anna. She'd go ballistic when she came back and discovered he'd disappeared.

"Let's wait for Anna. Or at least, let's find her."

"Not a chance." Johnny laughed. "The great Jeremy Masterson hiding behind the skirts of a woman. A Native, at that. This is one for the tabloids."

"You aren't thinking clearly. Anna—"

"You aren't thinking at all." Johnny cocked the pistol. "She can find you gone—or dead."

Jeremy didn't doubt that Johnny would pull the trigger. As he'd deduced earlier, he would be less of a liability and more convenient dead. He walked in the direction Johnny indicated.

"Hey." Johnny stopped him. "I wasn't going to tell you, but this should make your day." He pulled a cell phone from his pocket. "Remember this? You left it on one of the packhorses that the posse picked up. The battery's dead, but Anna won't know that." He ripped the battery out and put the phone on a rock. "I made a little note, too." He unfolded a piece of paper. "It says, 'I got tired of waiting and decided to use my ace. See you in Kerrville.' What do you think?" He stuck it under the useless phone.

Jeremy didn't answer. He didn't have to. Johnny's laughter filled the void. Anna would think he'd betrayed her and called for help, leaving her alone in the blistering hills.

Chapter Fourteen

Anna saw the rusted tin roof through heat that wavered in front of her eyes. Her throat was parched and her feet were burning, but her eyes were still good. The old Rivers's homestead was still standing. This was a place where she'd be welcomed, if anyone still lived here. This family had known and loved Thunder Horse.

Walking closer, Anna shaded her eyes with her hand. It was hard to see through the shimmering heat, but the place looked abandoned. She hurried forward as fast as her tired legs would carry her. It was nearly eleven o'clock, but the sun felt more like it was two in the afternoon.

The first sign of life was a dusty rooster that flew out of an old rusted car. The bird flapped its wings, threatened her, then flew away.

She was about to call out, when the front door burst open. The woman who came out was holding a shotgun that looked as if it weighed as much as she did.

"Hello," Anna called out. "I need help."

"You sure do if you've come all the way out here," the woman said. She didn't lower the gun a notch.

"My friend and I are stranded, and he's been

clawed up by a mountain lion.'' She searched the old woman's countenance for a hint of compassion or concern. The only emotion she recognized was wariness.

"Uh-huh," the woman answered. "That's none of my affair."

"I need to get him to a doctor."

"There's one in Kerrville and others beyond that."

Anna felt her exasperation threaten to explode. "I know where the doctors are, but I need some help in getting my friend there."

"This ain't no ambulance service, and for all I know you could be lying through your teeth."

"My grandfather taught me not to lie." She looked directly into the woman's eyes. "He said that a lie was like a cut in the heart. Eventually, it would rupture and blood would spill."

The barrel of the gun lowered slowly. "Thunder Horse."

"I'm his granddaughter, Anna Red Shoes. I need your help." She was relieved to see the old woman relax a bit.

"Where's this injured friend of yours?"

"About six miles west of here. Longer by the road." She looked around. There were no phone lines into the homestead. No power lines, either. "Do you have a vehicle?"

"If you want to call it that." The old woman laughed. "There's a truck in the shed out there. I use it to get supplies if the delivery gets held up."

Anna wanted to hug her. "Can I have some water, too?"

"Now that's easy enough." She signaled Anna inside.

In fifteen minutes, Anna had water, bread and

cheese, and the keys to the old beat-up pickup. She turned to the woman, who said her name was Elissa. "I'm in trouble. I have to tell you this. I've been accused of murdering a man in Kerrville."

"I thought it was you."

Anna's eyebrows shot up.

"No television, but I've got a radio. They gave a pretty good description of you. And the man. That writer fella, right?"

Anna nodded. "If I'm arrested I may not be able to bring the truck back."

"Leave the key under the floor mat. I'll find a way down to get it. Some of my bunch come up here every Tuesday to check on me." She laughed. "If I was a younger woman, I might be tempted to turn you in and go for that reward they're offering."

"Somehow, I don't think that's true." Whatever Elissa's goal in life, it certainly wasn't wealth. She'd long ago made the choice of living a life where money would always be a rare commodity.

"Well, if you do get caught, mention my name on the news. I've never been on the radio."

"That's a promise," Anna said, getting into the cab of the truck. It looked as if it might have come off the original Ford assembly line. To her surprise, it cranked like a charm.

The drive back to Jeremy took what seemed like hours, and Anna pressed the gas as hard as she dared over the treacherous road. Concern for Jeremy rode with her like a passenger in the truck.

But now they had a ride, a way to get to someplace safe.

Finally she pulled up as close to the rocks as she could get, and left the truck running. No way was she going to turn off the old antique and risk it's not starting again.

Jumping from the cab, she hurried forward. The water and some bread and cheese had refreshed her, and she scrambled quickly over the rocks.

At first she didn't believe her eyes. The secluded spot was empty. Jeremy was gone.

She searched among the big stones, thinking he'd crawled into the shelter of one to escape the heat. But after ten minutes, she had to accept that he was gone. She slowly turned around, looking in all directions. At last she saw the cell phone.

She went to it, picking it up slowly, as if it were a device the likes of which she'd never seen before. The back panel slid off, revealing the empty battery slot. The note fluttered to her feet and she retrieved it, reading the message three times before she lowered it.

He'd had the phone all the time. As soon as she was out of sight, he'd called for help. He didn't know if she'd found water or not. And he didn't care. He'd gotten himself rescued and left a useless phone—one he'd deliberately made inoperable—for her to find.

She hurled the phone against a rock, watching as it cracked into small pieces. The action gave her no satisfaction.

The words of the note were like a slap. ''I got tired of waiting.''

It was more infuriating than a slap.

And to think that she'd fallen for all of his fine talk—hook, line and sinker. The bitterness was almost unbearable. She knew he was capable of lies, yet she'd believed him.

The anger was so strong that she had to lean against a rock for support. When would she ever learn? He'd

stirred feelings in her that were real and special. She'd
allowed him to get closer to her heart than any man
she'd ever known. She had hugged the snake to her
bosom, and now she was surprised because she'd been
bitten.

She was a fool!

As mad as she was at him, though, she was doubly
angry with herself.

Pushing herself off from the rock, she started back
toward the truck. Now she had to figure out her next
move. Jeremy had undoubtedly gone back to Kerrville,
and there was no telling what he might say or do. He'd
said he was going to help clear her. Then again, he'd
also said he wanted to go to Mexico with her.

"Damn him."

In the stillness of the midday heat, the sound of the
truck motor suddenly stopping was as loud as a shout.
Anna scrambled over the rocks, her feet sliding in her
panic. When she got to the road, she saw the truck.
Sprinting to it, she climbed into the cab.

The keys were gone.

Fear chilled the perspiration on her body. Almost
afraid to do so, she looked around. She half expected
to see someone standing outside the cab. Instead, she
saw only rocks and the wild terrain of the hills.

Yet someone *had* sneaked up, stolen the keys and
dashed off. Her gaze scanned the vista. They could be
anywhere.

Watching.

She knew then exactly how a mouse feels when the
cat has it cornered.

JEREMY WASN'T SURPRISED when Johnny turned his
truck south, away from Verde Hill and southwest of

Kerrville. They were headed for Mexico. Or at least that general vicinity.

"The sheriff and posse are east of here," he said.

Johnny didn't answer.

"Will you let me call them and make sure Anna is picked up safely? She doesn't have a weapon. They need to know that."

"She'll be fine."

"Maria will get her?" Jeremy was tormented by thoughts of Anna, alone, without water or food or protection.

"You've got a lot of questions."

"How about one more, about you?" Jeremy decided to change tactics. "Is it really the money you're after, or is it something else? If it's money, maybe we can work something out."

He didn't have two hundred thousand dollars, but if his books were selling the way Ellie said, he'd have the money eventually. He'd part with all of the money he ever hoped to make just to know that Anna was safe.

Glancing out the corner of his eye, Johnny laughed. "Now you're going to offer to give me money to let you go?"

Johnny's open amusement made Jeremy want to punch him. The only thing that stopped him was the gun in Johnny's lap. His hand was on the grip and one finger was curled around the trigger. Jeremy wasn't willing to risk getting shot just to vent his anger.

"I don't have the cash, but I can get it. And I will give it to you. Just turn around, and let's get Anna. I'll go willingly wherever you want to take me. Just don't leave her back there without food or water or transportation."

"By about this time, she's mad enough at you to give her the strength to run back to Verde Hill," Johnny said. "That worthless phone and that note will have her boiling."

"Why does it give you such pleasure to torment her?"

Johnny slid a glance at him. "Okay, Mr. Writer, I'll tell you the truth. She had everything I ever wanted. She grew up with Thunder Horse. She knew the stories and the history of her people. And what does she do? She runs off to college to study the white man's ways. She has the blood to lead, yet she spends her time talking to men and women who only want to hurt each other. She puts herself in the line of fire every day as a counselor at that home for battered women. A noble job, right? Well, most of the time it doesn't make a bit of difference. She's wasting her life when she could be doing something important, leading her people to a new future."

"What's wrong with her choice of work?" Jeremy didn't understand.

"We need her."

Jeremy finally understood. "Your people?"

"Yeah. *Her* people. They just happen to be mine, too."

Jeremy felt the pulse jump in his neck. "Anna has a right to whatever life she chooses. You can't judge her decision."

"That's where you're wrong. I can, and I did. I knew when she told us that she was going to Kerrville to confront you that it was just an excuse."

Johnny's hands tightened on the wheel, and Jeremy was uncomfortably aware of the tension in him. He was high-strung and half-cocked.

"An excuse for what? Surely you don't think Anna murdered Henry Mills?"

Johnny snorted with disgust. "Of course not. Anna couldn't deliberately harm a fly. It was an excuse to see you. To talk to you. Maria didn't get it, but I knew. Anna's read everything you've ever written. She's a big fan. She said she wanted to make you understand how wrong you were in your book, but it wasn't that at all. She wanted to meet you."

"That's not true."

Johnny gave a snort of contempt. "You wouldn't know the truth if it bit you."

"I do know that Anna came to the store and made a scene bad enough that the customers left. She wasn't there as a fan, Johnny. She was angry."

"But not angry enough to leave you behind when you were injured—after you'd managed to set her up for a murder charge."

"Anna wouldn't have left anyone behind. Not even the writer who inaccurately portrayed her grandfather."

In the silence that stretched between them, Jeremy thought he might have reached Johnny. The one thing he knew for certain was that he'd always viewed the problems between the Natives and the settlers who'd taken over the land as an historical problem. Well, he'd certainly been naive and stupid. There was nothing ancient or dated about the man who held him at gunpoint.

They'd reached the bottom of a ravine, and Johnny slowed the truck, pulling over to the edge of the road.

A small creek cut through the bottom, amber water sparkling through trees that were just beginning to bud with green leaves. By Jeremy's best guess, they'd

leave the Hill Country behind in a matter of miles.
Then the flatlands would stretch down to the Mexican
border.

As rough and harsh as the hills were, the flats could
be equally unforgiving. Pastures for animals were
scarce, and water was a rare commodity.

"Get out," Johnny said.

Jeremy thought for a minute that he'd misunder-
stood him.

Johnny's finger pulled back the hammer of the gun.
"Go on and get out," he said in a sharper voice.

Jeremy's first thought was that Johnny intended to
kill him; wanted Jeremy out of the truck so he could
shoot him. He hesitated.

"If you don't get out of the truck, I'll shoot you in
the foot." Johnny pointed the gun down at the floor-
board where Jeremy's feet rested.

"What's this all about?"

"You're not in a position to ask questions. Just do
what you're told."

The hinges of the door gave a raw squall as Jeremy
opened it. He got out. Now that the truck wasn't moving, the heat was suffocating.

"Close the door," Johnny said. He still sat behind
the wheel.

Jeremy slammed the door.

"I wouldn't wander too far from the road. It was
chilly up in the hills, but down here the rattlers will
be crawling." Johnny laughed as he gunned the gas.

The truck tires snatched at the loose gravel, spraying
it behind the vehicle. In a cloud of hot dust, Johnny
Severe drove away.

IT WAS A LONG WALK back to the Rivers's place, but
Anna didn't know where else to go. She'd tried to hot-

wire the truck, but her knowledge of theft techniques wasn't up to par. There was a slim chance that Elissa Rivers would have a spare key.

But Anna walked mostly with the need to keep moving. She felt as if every step she made were being watched. If she kept moving, eventually she'd come to a place where she might catch sight of her stalker. Or at least, that's what she had to hope.

So far there'd been no sign of anyone. She'd even begun to hope that she might be captured by the posse. If they didn't shoot her, they'd have to give her water and a ride back to Kerrville.

It was almost amusing. She was stranded—a sitting duck waiting to be arrested by the posse. Jeremy had probably already told them where to hunt for her.

Bitterness welled up in her throat. She'd believed everything he'd said. It was obvious the man was a sociopath. He lied for the sake of lying. And he played games with people for some sick amusement.

Well, she'd learned her lesson this time. If she made it back to civilization in one piece, her first action would be to go to the sheriff and turn herself in. No legal punishment could be worse than what she'd endured during the past twenty-four hours.

She forced her feet to keep moving, ignoring her body's complaints. Her grandfather had roamed these very hills, hiding and running from the men who relentlessly chased him. He'd survived. She would, too.

She climbed the hill in front of her and stopped on the crest. Below her, the road was a light yellow against the darker rust of the hills. She heard the vehicle long before she saw the sleek automobile. It was moving slowly.

For a split second Anna hesitated. She could see enough to know that there was one person in the car—a woman.

Lifting her hands and shouting, Anna started down the slope toward the road. ''Hey!'' she called out. ''Hey! Wait for me.'' She didn't know anyone who would drive such an expensive car—and certainly no member of the posse would be in a Lexus.

To her immense relief, the car slowed to a halt. She scampered down the hill, half running and half sliding, the gravel avalanching along with her.

The tinted window of the car eased down to reveal a blond woman.

Anna tried to slow her descent, but the incline was too steep. She sat down and slid the rest of the way, halting almost at the fender of the car. When she looked up, she recognized the woman as the owner of the bookstore: Ellie Clark.

The coincidence that the carefully made-up bookstore owner was out in the hills was too much to believe. Anna stared at the woman, her heart hammering.

''Where's Jeremy?'' the woman asked. She looked up toward the incline as if she expected the writer to be there.

''I don't know.'' Anna kept her voice level, without the surge of anger she felt at the thought of the man.

''You left with him.'' The tone was accusatory. ''The two of you have led Lem and his trackers on one heck of a chase.'' She glanced behind Anna. ''So where is he?''

There was no reason to lie, especially not to Ellie. But she didn't have to be specific, either. ''He was in some rocks, resting. I went to get help. When I came back, he was gone.''

Anna dusted her jeans, using that as an excuse to walk closer to the car so that she could see inside. Ellie's hands were on the steering wheel. The seat beside her was empty.

"How did you know to come here?" Anna asked.

"You and Jeremy left an easy trail to follow." Ellie arched an eyebrow. "Loose horses, blood, a wrecked truck. Anything I missed?"

If the trail had been that easy to follow, the sheriff and his men would be here, too. The telephone Jeremy had left was clear evidence of what had occurred. "Jeremy called you to rescue him. You've taken him into town and now you're back for me."

Ellie shook her head. "I haven't seen him. He was supposed to call last night. But I guess he couldn't when he left his cell phone in his saddlebag. I was shocked when Blane caught those runaway horses and pulled out his phone. Up until then, I figured it was one of his famous, wild escapades. I mean, he told me he was going to catch Henry's killer, and that you were the killer. It was sort of crazy, but that was Jeremy. And we both knew how such a coup would pump his book sales sky high." Ellie shrugged. "Then, when Blane found the horses and the phone, I thought Jeremy might be in real trouble."

Anna digested that information. "The phone was on the packhorses when they got away, and the members of the posse found it?" So how did it get back to Jeremy? Anna's stomach knotted with sudden concern, but she knew better than to show any emotion. Ellie claimed to be Jeremy's accomplice. But Anna had learned not to trust anyone completely.

"Yes, the posse had it. And then it disappeared again." Ellie's blue eyes were sharp and speculative. "Why are you so interested in that phone?"

"Your writer friend has a lot of tricks up his sleeve. The disappearing and reappearing phone seems to be one of his favorites." It wasn't a real answer, but it was all Anna was going to give. Until she figured out the mess, she wasn't volunteering any information.

"Really, Anna, tell me where Jeremy is. I can help both of you."

"I don't know," Anna answered. And she didn't. It was obvious that he'd met someone in the rocks. And judging from the note, it was someone he'd expected to meet. Since the phone came from the posse, it had to be someone who'd been hunting him. Whatever Jeremy was up to, he'd pulled it off. He'd played her like a fiddle at a Saturday night dance. Probably material for another bestselling book, just as Ellie had implied.

"Will you take me back to Kerrville?" Anna asked abruptly. "The sooner I get there, the sooner I can start to straighten a few things out."

"So you're planning on turning yourself in?"

Anna nodded, aware of a strange undercurrent in Ellie's voice. "I didn't do anything wrong. I'm not afraid of the law."

"Most folks who run have something to hide." Ellie leaned out the window, her gaze roving over Anna. "I just want to make sure you aren't armed. Seems to me that if you did kill Henry, you just might have killed Jeremy, too. His body may be somewhere up there in those hills."

"You can be sure that if Jeremy Masterson is dead around here, his body will be here for the next few months. He's too damn mean for a wild animal to eat.''

Ellie pointed at the passenger door. ''Get in. If you want a ride to town, I'll take you.''

Anna walked around the car and got in the passenger seat. ''I want to talk to the sheriff,'' she said.

Ellie didn't say anything as she put the car in gear and pressed the gas pedal.

The scenery flashed by the window, and Anna felt her body go limp in the air-conditioned car. She'd never felt anything as good as the cool air jetting out of the vents. She leaned back in the leather seats and let the car gobble up the hard miles.

''Are you sure you want to go to Kerrville?'' Ellie asked.

''I'd like to go home,'' Anna said. ''I'd prefer to go back in time three days, back to the moment I decided to go to Jeremy's book signing in your store and make a scene. I'd squelch that whole plan, and right now I'd be at my job, doing what I should be doing.''

Ellie laughed softly. ''That was some scene. You single-handedly set yourself up as the type of woman who was wild enough to commit murder.''

Anna didn't say anything, but she knew that her heritage had as much to do with that perception as did her behavior. It was a point she didn't have the energy to make.

''Where did you leave Jeremy?'' Ellie asked for the third time.

''You mean his body?'' Anna asked, not bothering to hide her sarcasm. ''I'll never tell.''

''I saw an old truck back up the road. That must have been the spot.''

Anna realized that the bookstore owner was a very

perceptive woman. Another tingle of warning stole over her. She shot a glance at Ellie. She was petite, very pretty, her appearance a work of art. But that didn't mean that she wasn't sharp as a whip. Anna had to concede that she, too, was guilty of basing opinions on appearance. She'd assumed that Ellie was a woman interested in looks and social graces. But there was a lot more to her.

"Is that where you left him?" Ellie pressed.

"What's your stake in this?" Anna asked, ignoring the question.

"I supported Jeremy when he couldn't sell a short story for pulp paper." Her small, manicured hands tightened on the steering wheel. "You could say that I've been his primary support. Now he's successful. I don't want to see him sabotage his career just as he's beginning to have one. You're turning yourself in. If Jeremy is up there somewhere, injured by a mountain lion, I want to call Lem and get the posse to pick him up. The longer this drags on, the harder it's going to be to stop."

Though there were obviously elements of truth in what the woman said, Anna didn't buy it entirely. Her intuition was on high alert. She had to be very, very careful how she answered this woman. Besides, she'd never mentioned how Jeremy had been injured.

"It doesn't matter where I left Jeremy. I told you, he's gone. I searched the area and there was no sign of him. He must have left in a vehicle."

"Oh?" Ellie looked away from the road and at her.

"His leg was badly injured from the cat attack. From what I could tell, it was getting infected. That's why I left him in the rocks and went for help. The truth is, if someone doesn't get him to a doctor soon, he could die.''

Ellie nodded, her hands tightening on the wheel. "I'm sure he's fine."

"There's not a chance he made it in to town?" Anna asked.

"Not to my knowledge." She pointed at the car phone in the console. "I'm sure if they'd found Jeremy, someone would have called me. I've been with that posse on and off for the last three days. Lem and all the others know that Jeremy is like a brother to me. I'm sure someone would have called. Or at least it would have been on the news."

She switched on the radio. A song concluded and the newscaster smoothly slid into the day's news.

"A posse of fifteen men and women continue to search the rough terrain of the Hill Country for suspected murderers Jeremy Masterson and Anna Red Shoes. Masterson, an acclaimed novelist, is wanted in the murder of his editor, Henry Mills. Red Shoes is believed to be an accomplice. They are to be viewed as armed and dangerous—"

Ellie clicked off the radio. "See, he didn't make it back." She took a deep breath. "I hope, for your sake, that he isn't dead. That would leave you in a real mess, wouldn't it?"

Chapter Fifteen

After an hour, Jeremy knew that he couldn't walk anymore. He'd had water from the small creek where Johnny had put him out of the truck. He'd drunk his fill, but had no way to carry any. Determined to get on the main road, to make progress toward being found, he'd left the water behind.

Now his leg was throbbing, blood and serum seeping through the dressing and the denim of his jeans. The heat was intolerable, and he knew it was his fever as much as the sun.

In all of his lust for writing experience, he'd never hoped to feel so truly helpless. He'd sought experience like the hunter he was. He'd survived danger and fear, but until now he'd never truly known desperation.

Johnny had put him out on a dead-end road and driven away. For the first half hour, Jeremy had assumed that someone would come along and pick him up. He'd assumed that Johnny was working in concert with Blane or Lem or some damn body.

For the last half hour, though, he had begun to think that Johnny had been smart enough to leave him out in the elements to let nature do the work. That would leave Johnny with the perfect setup—a dead man with a bounty on his head.

Even better, a man dead by natural causes.

A wave of dizziness made him stumble. Jeremy wanted to laugh. It would be ironic if he lost consciousness in the middle of the road and was killed by a vehicle sent to rescue him. Now that would be a fitting end to the entire mess.

Up ahead he saw a stand of the scrub cedars that were so often the bane of ranchers. To him, they looked like an oasis. It was unlikely that water would be found there, but it was worth a look. Besides, he had to find shade. He was burning up.

He stumbled off the rough path and began the slow trek to the trees. At last he reached them and sank down in the shade. He'd look for water a little later. First he had to sit for a while.

Even sitting, he was dizzy. He leaned back against a rock. At first he thought he was hallucinating when he heard a vehicle engine. Maybe Anna actually had found some means of transportation. He tried to get up—but he couldn't.

The vehicle was coming fast, and he knew he had to get closer to the road, otherwise, no one would see him. He forced himself up, but his injured leg gave way beneath him, and he fell. Pulling himself up on one of the tree trunks, he saw the flash of a truck.

''Hey!'' he called, as the vehicle rounded a bend. ''Hey!'' He tried to wave and nearly fell again. He thought he recognized the female driver, the pretty brunette he'd taken to the party as his date. He had to be hallucinating!

The truck sped off with a metallic glint, and along with it went all hope of rescue. He knew what had happened, the scenario playing out in his head just as Johnny had planned it. Anna would not be looking for him. She'd gone back to the circle of rocks for him, found the telephone and note, and gone on. To safety, he hoped. But everyone would think that he was with her.

Jeremy leaned back against the rock and closed his eyes. Sweat trickled down his face, and he was too tired to wipe it away. The only sensible thing to do was sleep. Maybe once he rested, he'd have the strength to make it back to the road.

ANNA FOCUSED ON not showing her thoughts, as Ellie's car sped toward Kerrville. The silence between the two women had grown long and uncomfortable, at least for Anna. She cast about in her mind for a topic of conversation that would allow her to probe the other woman. She wasn't certain what Ellie's role in any of this was, but with each passing mile she grew more and more concerned.

"How did you meet Jeremy?" Anna finally asked.

"Like most writers, he's an avid reader." Ellie answered. "Awful taste in literature. Either those tormented Russians or Tom Clancy. His taste in reading material reflects his philosophy of life—one extreme or the other. There's no middle ground for Jeremy."

Anna couldn't determine the underlying emotion in Ellie's voice. Was her talk of extremes a signal that she believed Jeremy capable of murder? She pressed on. "Do you know him well?"

"Well enough. We've been friends for more than ten years. Of course, friendship with Jeremy, or any writer, is a twisting road. The work is always first, you know."

There was definitely jealousy in Ellie's voice. Anna couldn't help but wonder at it. "I've never given that aspect of writing much thought."

"Well, before you fall in love with him—as most women do—think about it. You can never compete with what's happening in his head."

The anger in Ellie's voice shook Anna—as did the harsh prediction. To cover her own unruly emotions, she decided on another tack—one that would undoubtedly prove to be a bomb. "Do you think he's capable of killing his editor?"

Ellie's reaction was stronger than Anna anticipated. The car swerved, almost going off the road. Anna started to grab for the wheel, but stopped herself.

Ellie got the vehicle under control before she answered.

"I seriously doubt Jeremy is guilty of killing Henry," she said, frowning as she cast a glance at Anna. "Writers, though, are unpredictable. Let's just say that Jeremy's not my *favorite* suspect."

"But you believe he could have done it?"

"Let's give him the benefit of the doubt, for the moment."

"So if I didn't kill Henry, and Jeremy didn't kill him, who did?" Anna pressed.

"I've been asking myself that question over and over." Ellie raised her eyebrows as she gave Anna a quick look. "It had to be someone with access to the house *and* to my bookstore, since your knife was stolen from there. Possibly someone who was at the book signing and saw me put the knife under the counter."

Anna nodded, listening closely. She'd been wondering how the knife had gotten from the bookstore to the murder scene.

"And it had to be someone who wanted to hurt either Jeremy or Henry—" Ellie gave her a speculative look "—unless it was someone you knew who is better than the CIA at Machiavellian manipulation. That would mean they deliberately set you up for a murder charge."

Anna shook her head. "I don't think so. I'm the coincidence in this plot. I just happened to be in the wrong place at the wrong time."

"Then we have to assume the murder stems from Jeremy."

Anna found that she agreed with Ellie's assessment. "Jeremy even thought perhaps he was the intended target of the murder."

"That makes sense."

"But who would want to kill Jeremy?"

"We're back to the original question," Ellie pointed out as she turned east at a fork in the road. Anna could tell they were getting closer to civilization. The road was better maintained, and along the side there was occasional fencing. It wouldn't be long before she would confront the law. If she had, at least, a theory of the murder, she would feel less apprehensive.

"Let me ask a personal question," Ellie said. "Did Jeremy ever talk to you about Lucinda?"

"A little." Anna had no desire to go into Jeremy's personal life, but Lucinda was a potential suspect.

"Then you know there's bad blood there. Lucinda was furious with Jeremy."

"Yes. He told me that."

"I doubt he told you her background." Ellie's laugh was bitter. "I doubt he knows. Men think that the past is never relevant to them. Everything begins and ends with them.''

Anna wasn't sure where all of this was going, but Ellie was talking, and the more she talked the better Anna was beginning to understand the dynamics of the situation. It was also very true that the past was never over. The past was part of the reason she was in this situation.

''Tell me about her,'' she said.

''Let me explain her history. She's a tramp with money. Money she took from an ex-husband, I should add. Was it her fourth or fifth? I forget. Anyway, she never worked a day in her life. She has no appreciation for work. Social power and wealth are the two goals of her life, and she usually relies on her feminine wiles to attain those.''

Anna didn't see the relevance. ''Ellie, there are plenty of women like her out there, but I don't see how this applies to what's happening now, unless you're saying Lucinda might be the murderer.''

Ellie's knuckles whitened on the wheel as she swung around a curve. ''Give me a chance. I don't think Lucinda killed anyone.''

''So what are you getting at?''

''Blane Griffin.'' Ellie lifted one eyebrow. ''I think Blane killed Henry, and I think he did it for two reasons.''

Anna felt a thrill of excitement. This was almost exactly what Jeremy had said. ''Yes, Jeremy thought of this! Blane wanted what Jeremy had. He was a man eaten alive with jealousy. And I think he killed Henry and decided to set Jeremy up to take the fall.''

Ellie held up a hand to stop Anna from talking.

"But you broke in on the murder scene and messed up the entire plan."

"Exactly!" Anna said, relieved that at last there was someone who was able to help sort out the facts. "Let's go to the sheriff and tell him this."

"Not so fast," Ellie said. "The problem is that I'm not sure Lem or anyone else will believe us. See, Blane's been riding with Lem and the posse. He's been getting them to see the facts the way he wants them to. They honestly believe that Jeremy might have killed Henry with your help." Ellie bit her bottom lip. "And I may be partially responsible for that."

"How?" Frustration made Anna's voice rough.

"I told them that Jeremy and Henry were at odds over Jeremy's writing—that the sequel wasn't going well. It was the truth, but I never realized how it might sound as evidence against Jeremy. And I had no idea that Blane and Henry were negotiating such a big book deal. I've given Jeremy motive for murder, when it should be Blane who's the suspect."

Anna couldn't hide her disappointment. Ellie was right. It sounded bad for Jeremy—and that was bad for her. "What *was* Henry Mills's reaction to the sequel? Was there trouble there?" Jeremy hadn't talked about it much, but she'd gotten the impression the book was going well.

Ellie hesitated. "Henry called up to the shop when Jeremy was doing his signing. He said for me not to disturb Jeremy, but that he was having some difficulty with the manuscript. He wanted Jeremy to call him after the signing was over. He sounded very worried."

"What was the problem?"

Ellie shrugged. "He wasn't specific, but he did urge me not to tell Jeremy there was anything wrong. He just wanted Jeremy to keep his temper in check, sign the books and get back to the ranch. Obviously they'd been having some disagreements.''

Anna was beginning to sketch out a picture in her head about the events of the day that Henry Mills was murdered. ''Henry was supposed to attend a party with Jeremy, right?''

''Yes. It was given by the Ketterings. They're big fans of Jeremy's and they'd arranged a lovely party to honor him and his books. Henry was invited, too, but after talking with him, I knew he wouldn't be socializing. He was down here to work—the publisher has a lot of money sunk into Jeremy. Enough that they sent an editor to work with an author, which is unheard of. Watershed House can't afford a bomb. And then at the book signing, I saw Jeremy shining up to that little brunette. I knew there was serious trouble with his writing, and he'd vowed to finish the book before he started dating again.''

Anna recognized the uncomfortable sensation of jealousy—she wanted to ask what brunette, but instead she kept on track. Her days of mooning over Jeremy were over. ''You think Jeremy left Henry at home deliberately?''

Ellie rubbed the corner of her eye. ''Jeremy hates public embarrassment. If he'd gone home to the ranch and talked with Henry, and if Henry truly didn't like the sequel, there would have been a fight. Jeremy would not have wanted Henry at the party that was meant as a celebration for him, especially not if there had been hard words. There's one additional fact. When Jeremy decides to charm a woman, that's all he wants to focus on.''

Anna felt as if hot water had been splashed on her

face. She felt the color flood up her cheeks, and prayed that Ellie wouldn't notice. She knew too well how attentive and charming Jeremy could be, when he chose to be.

"You weren't at the party. You missed the scene with Lucinda. I warned him about her. I tried to tell him that if he dumped her on the curb along with his other castoffs, there was going to be hell to pay."

Anna forced herself to listen, even as she felt her heart begin to close toward Jeremy. Ellie was recounting the facts as if they were old and uninteresting. But this was a side of Jeremy that Anna had shut her eyes to. A side she now had to force herself to see. This was the lesson her grandfather had tried to teach her. She'd failed to listen to her instincts and had led with her heart. Even knowing what Jeremy had written about Thunder Horse, how he'd refused to even listen to her, she'd allowed herself to fall in love with him. A few nights together, the fear and worry of being pursued—those things had eroded her good sense. She'd let herself care about a man who bent the truth whenever it suited him.

The hardest truth of all was that Jeremy could have stopped the events of the past few days whenever he'd chosen to do so. He'd had the damn phone when he'd been injured by the lion. And he hadn't used it. That indicated just how hardheaded—and selfish—he could be.

Ellie cast Anna a curious glance, but continued to talk. "You knew that Blane and Jeremy were once best friends? They grew up together. They've played together since they were in the first grade. Jeremy taught Blane all he knows about tracking and outdoor skills. There was always a rivalry between them. Jeremy was the quarterback and Blane was the wide receiver. Blane was the math whiz and Jeremy loved biology.''

''You sound like you've known them both a long time.'' Anna knew her voice sounded dead, but Ellie was too busy now to notice.

Ellie shook her head. ''No, but I've heard this from a lot of people. Kerrville is a small town. The bookstore is a gathering place for writers and readers. That's a pretty select group within the broader society.''

''Go on, please.''

''When Blane started writing, Jeremy had to do it, too.''

''Blane started first?'' This was surprising.

''Yes, and that's what makes it doubly hard for him, or so I've been told. Jeremy would never have written a word if not for Blane's interest in it. Add Lucinda Estar into the mess and you've got the ingredients for serious trouble.''

Anna couldn't agree more. The finger of guilt pointed more and more at Blane Griffin as the murderer. Even as she sorted through the new information Ellie had given her, she couldn't suppress a worry for Jeremy. Where had he gone? More important, why had he left in the manner that he had? Those were questions only Jeremy could answer.

She refocused her thoughts on the murder. ''Ellie, do you know if the coroner had put a time of death on Mr. Mills?''

Ellie shot her a quick look. ''I'm not privy to that kind of information. Lem knows I'm a good friend of Jeremy's. He won't tell me a damn thing.''

''I thought it might have have been on the news,''

Anna explained. "Do you know if Blane has been with the posse this whole time?" Someone had been shooting at them, had stolen the key to the old truck. If Blane was with the posse, that would rule him out.

"Blane's a tracker. He's been out there most of the time."

Anna didn't point out that often the tracker rode miles ahead. And as she'd just learned the hard way, a man with a cell phone could do a lot of business—even in the middle of isolation.

"Where is Lucinda now?"

"Who the hell knows? She rode out with the posse, dressed like Annie Oakley and carrying an elephant rifle." Ellie laughed. "With any luck she tried to fire the thing and it knocked her back in a dry gulch somewhere."

"Is she a marksman?" Ellie clearly didn't suspect Lucinda, but Anna wasn't so sure the redhead hadn't had a hand in some of the misfortune that had befallen her.

"Jeremy taught her to shoot. If I had to guess, I'd say she was pretty good."

Anna glanced out the window. The terrain had become much softer. They were almost out of the ravines and high hills. In another few minutes they would be on the main highway to Kerrville, and she would find out what fate had in store for her.

"Anna, I want you to rethink giving yourself up," Ellie said gently.

Anna didn't answer. Up ahead was a stop sign and a paved intersection.

"Jeremy's up to something. Why don't we wait and see what he does?" Ellie pressed.

"I'm not inclined to put my future into his hands."

Anna tried not to show the pain she felt. She'd already put her trust in Jeremy once—and he'd tricked her. "I think it would be best to go ahead and talk with the sheriff."

"I wouldn't sacrifice myself for him." There was a warning in Ellie's voice.

"I'm not. Don't worry about that. It's just that I think it would be best for me to turn myself in, before someone else does. Guilt is often created by perception. If I come forward, at least the perception will be that I'm not running. You pointed that out yourself. As far as Jeremy is concerned…" She shrugged.

"You honestly don't know where he is?"

"If I did, I'd tell the sheriff and let the posse bring him in."

Ellie brought the car to a stop at the intersection. "So you don't know if he's hiding up in one of those caves?"

"He could be in Mexico," Anna said. "For all I know, this whole business of a bounty from his publisher could have been his plan, and he's sitting in a bar drinking tequila and having a blast." Anna let her full exasperation show.

"Listen to me. Don't give yourself up. Not yet. Why don't we wait and see what he's going to do?" One corner of Ellie's mouth lifted in a smile. "Look at it this way. Now he doesn't know where *you* are. He thinks he left you back in the middle of nowhere. If he wants to play vanishing games, let's give him a dose of his own medicine. Besides, your best defense is in being free and working to find the real killer. And I'll help you."

The appeal was instant. Anna nodded. "You may be on to something."

"I have a cabin on the Guadeloupe River. You can stay there until we decide what to do."

It was a generous offer, but one, Anna knew, that could spell trouble for Ellie. "I don't know. That would make you an accomplice in my flight from the law."

"Fiddle-faddle." Ellie turned the car west. "I'm not afraid of Lem."

"This isn't just a local thing. It's gotten much bigger. The national media are involved—"

"True, but Lem will have to be the one to charge me with accessory to murder, and I don't think he has the stomach for that. I'm a pillar of the community." Ellie laughed. "And I haven't had this much excitement in a long time."

"Okay." Anna felt a nagging worry. She'd made up her mind to turn herself in, and that had seemed like the best route. Now, here she was getting sidetracked by another plan.

But Ellie was smart. Perhaps it was worthwhile waiting a bit longer.

"The cabin has everything you need," Ellie said, pressing the accelerator as the luxury car spun down the paved road. "There's even cable television so you can keep up with your growing notoriety. This morning they had a radio interview with the director of the shelter where you work."

"Oh, no." Anna felt another corner of her world crumble.

"It was positive. Mrs. Greenwald thinks you're the best. She said you absolutely couldn't be involved in murder."

"That's a plus, I suppose."

"When this is all over and your name is cleared,

there shouldn't be a problem with your job. I'd be willing to bet my store on that.''

Anna didn't answer. For one blazing second she was mad enough at Jeremy to tie him in a knot. It was because of him that she was here. And there was no telling what *he* was doing right this minute. Or whether he even cared about the havoc he'd wrought.

Chapter Sixteen

At the sound of the bird's raucous cry, Jeremy forced his eyes open. He felt as if he'd been asleep for years, except that he was still exhausted. The effort of making his eyelids lift was almost more than he could endure. The insistent bird wouldn't let him rest, though. He tried to focus on the hellacious creature and realized that his eyes weren't working properly. The bird was enormous—far too big to be a crow.

"Get," he said, wanting the animal to leave him alone and let him sleep. "Get out of here before I shoot you."

"Big talk for such a sick man."

He thought he was dreaming. The old woman's voice sounded as if it came from inside his head. His eyes tried to find her, but he saw only tree trunks and rocks.

"You get away from me, too," he whispered. "Just get on."

"Bossy, aren't you?"

He almost choked on the water that suddenly dribbled on his lips.

"Even a baby bird knows enough to open its mouth. Open up."

He obeyed the sharp command, and the cool water trickled onto his parched tongue. He realized he was thirsty. Very thirsty. He started to gulp the water, then felt a firm hand on his chest, pushing him back.

"Bossy and greedy. Just hold your horses. Take it a little at a time, while I try to figure out what to do with you."

The water seemed to help his vision, and he finally focused on the old woman. She was petite but wiry. For all of her age and small stature, he could see she was strong. "Who are you?" he asked.

"Nobody you'd know, Mr. Writer. I been listenin' to the news stories about you. There's a big reward for turnin' you in."

Jeremy had a vague recollection of something about money and a posse, but he couldn't remember how it applied to him. "Where am I?"

"By the looks of you, I'd say hell would be a good description. But things are starting to look up for you."

Jeremy suddenly remembered Anna. He tried to sit up and hunt for her, but the old woman pushed him back down. He was weak as the proverbial kitten.

"My friend—she went for help. She's out here somewhere..." He cast his head from side to side, but the only thing he saw was the big black bird sitting perched in a cedar tree. It was an enormous bird. Ugly. If he could only make his eyes focus properly.

"I saw the girl. She took my truck and then left it by the side of the road. Looked to me like she went to get something from the Stone Circle."

It was coming back to Jeremy. He'd been waiting for Anna in a circle of rocks, a safe place. Except that Johnny had found him.

"We have to find Anna," he said.

"I'm a lucky old woman." She gave him more water, this time allowing him to drink from a tin cup. "When I left the house, I thought to bring the spare key to the truck." The old woman laughed. "Your luck is getting better, too, I'd say. You've got a ride, and from the looks of that leg, you won't be walkin' far."

"Where is she?" Jeremy tried to hold the fear down, but he wasn't successful.

"Can't rightly say. But there was no blood, so she either left voluntarily or didn't have time to put up much of a fight."

Even the idea was enough to make Jeremy try once again to get up. When he did, he felt the lightning bolt of pain in his leg. He tried to smother the groan, but didn't quite manage it.

"Your leg's in a bad way. If we can't do something to stop that infection, you're going to end up with a stump."

Jeremy believed her. He got his elbows under him enough to sit up halfway. The sight of his leg made him want to gag. "I need a doctor."

"You're goin' to get one. But first I have to get you to the truck. That means you're going to have to put all of your strength into getting from here to there. Once you're in the truck, you can faint or scream or do whatever you want. Just don't waste the energy on that foolishness until you're in the cab."

The old woman wasn't exactly comforting, but she was practical. "How did you find me?" he asked. He took another sip of the water she held out to him. With each swallow, things were becoming clearer.

"I had a vision," she said. "In my vision a young

man I used to know stopped by. He was looking for a beautiful woman, too. He was a man filled with jealousy and hate and envy, and he confessed that he'd left an injured man to die.''

Jeremy cut his eyes to look at her. She didn't look crazy. Old and worn, but not crazy. ''Was the man in this vision named Johnny Severe?'' he asked.

''Who knows? Dream images never have real names.''

''How did you know who I am.''

''I was listening to my old radio. That's all I have up to the house, an old radio. I never held much with television. Anyway, I heard all about this famous writer who most likely murdered his editor. It sounded like a good yarn to me, so I listened on and heard how there was money to be made for the person who found the writer and turned him in.''

''I wouldn't believe that,'' Jeremy said, suddenly aware that he was at this stranger's mercy. She could as easily knock him in the head as help him. ''Talk is cheap.''

''Maybe so. I reckon if you die, I can drive your body into town and try to collect.'' She paused. ''I had another vision earlier this week. A man you know.''

''And who would that be?'' Jeremy asked. She was stronger than him *and* his only means of transportation, but he was finding it hard to take the old woman seriously. She seemed a little loony.

''An old Native man. Name of Thunder Horse.'' She grinned at his involuntary reaction. ''I see you know him.''

''In the last two days, he's begun to figure prominently in my life.''

"I'll bet. Anyway, Thunder Horse told me to expect you. He said you had things to learn from me."

"Next, you'll be saying he also wanted an apology for my book."

"He was never the kind of man to ask for an apology. He figured if one was needed, the offending party would know enough to give it."

"What did you say your name was?" Jeremy had a sudden thought that maybe Anna had sent the old woman.

"I never said. It ain't important. Truth be told, mister, I'd be more worried about my woman and my leg, in that order. Anna Red Shoes isn't the kind to leave an injured man."

Jeremy felt the worry like a wave washing over his entire body. It was true. Anna would never have abandoned him to die of infection or thirst. "You have to show me where the truck was left. We have to search for her." Even as he talked, he knew he was worse than useless. The old woman would do a lot better without him along.

"I looked pretty thoroughly. There wasn't a sign of her. You're just lucky I decided to follow up on my vision and come lookin' for you. 'Course, I didn't have any specific directions, but once I got in the general vicinity, I followed him—" She pointed to the nearest cedar.

Jeremy followed the direction of her finger and saw the bird. It gave one more loud cry and then flapped enormous wings and lifted slowly into the air. Jeremy took a deep breath. It was a buzzard. The old woman had followed the carrion bird. He felt the hair on the back of his neck tingle as he realized how very close to death he'd been. The bird had known. It had given up the slow flight of circles that was the traditional behavior for a buzzard waiting for something to die, and had already settled into the cedar.

Had the old woman not arrived, he would have been buzzard delight in a matter of hours.

ELLIE'S RIVER CABIN was filled with books and light and the finest bathroom Anna had ever seen. She availed herself of the tub with massaging jets, foaming bubble bath and a glass of wine. Sinking back into the hot water, Anna felt as if she were in paradise.

It was a momentary respite from her reeling emotions and from reality, but she savored it as she sipped the wine and washed her hair and skin.

She was able to hold her worries at bay until she'd toweled herself dry and combed her hair. But standing at the mirror and staring at her reflection, she found she had to confront the truth.

She was alone in a stranger's home. Ellie had gone back to town, promising Anna that she would talk with the sheriff and try to regain control of a situation that had become a media feeding frenzy. Ellie was working on her behalf.

And Jeremy? It was his injury that nagged at Anna. She was over her initial burst of anger at him for leaving her with a useless phone and a stupid note. She was stuck with one question. Why? She'd scouted the area where she'd left him and there hadn't been signs of a struggle. But then, Jeremy hadn't really been strong enough to put up a fight.

She combed the tangles out of her dark hair and faced herself again in the ornate mirror. Jeremy Masterson had made her believe in him, as a person and as a man. For the two nights they'd been together, she

had felt something for him that was more than interest
or appreciation for his talent. She'd seen behind the
facade of the macho man, the cooler-than-cool writer.
She'd seen a man of keen intellect and good character.

Or had she seen what she wanted to see? Had Jeremy purposely acted like the mirror, giving back the
image she expected?

Surely it was the art of a con man to make the mark
believe in the snake oil. Perhaps Jeremy was nothing
more than a literary con man.

Anna studied her reflection. She peered deep into
her own dark eyes and sought the truth. She saw her
doubt there, her fear and unwillingness to be hurt by
a man who had the potential to genuinely break her
heart.

And behind the fear she saw her own desire to prove
this man to be worthy of her heart.

She leaned forward and pressed her forehead to the
mirror, closing her eyes and sighing. Now that her
temper had subsided she was left to face some of the
questions she should have asked earlier. It was only
by answering these questions that she would know the
right path to take.

Who *was* Jeremy Masterson?

She'd seen him with two faces, but which was real?
Her heart told her one thing and her brain told her
another.

The problem was that she couldn't pursue one without risking the other. With the cool glass of the mirror
against her face, she made her decision.

Her mind could tolerate a mistake a lot more easily
than could her heart—but love wasn't worth the effort
if a woman wasn't willing to take a risk. The smart
thing to do was to hide out at Ellie's and wait until

the air cleared. But if her heart was right, Jeremy might be in danger. Which meant that she couldn't afford to wait.

She walked out of the bathroom and looked at the queen-size bed draped with an elegant coverlet and plumped with goose-down pillows. From the first moment she'd seen it, she'd anticipated crawling beneath the cool cotton sheets and sleeping.

That wasn't going to happen, though. She knew it even as she slipped into the clean clothes Ellie had put out for her. Business clothes—not her usual jeans and cotton blouses.

The bookstore owner had been more than generous, and Anna felt slightly guilty as she started down the stairs. But she couldn't stay in the house without knowing for certain what had happened to Jeremy.

Ellie had said the Explorer in the drive was hers to use if she wanted it. Anna went outside and climbed inside. When she reached to find the keys, she realized that Ellie, in her haste to get back to town, had forgotten to leave them.

Anna went back inside, found the telephone book and looked up a car rental agency. There was no way to rent a vehicle without giving a credit card—which was an invitation to the posse to come and get her. Ellie had a car phone, but Anna had no idea what the number was. She tapped her finger on the phone book. The only person she could call was Maria. Besides, she owed her friend a phone call to let her know she was safe but still a long way from Mexico.

She lifted the receiver and started to dial. There was only a strange echo on the line. Anna tried several times but couldn't get a dial tone. The shiver that crept up her spine was a warning.

Not bothering with the inside phones, she went out and traced the phone lines into the house. The box was on the north side, and Anna wasn't surprised when she saw the lines had been severed. The footprints in the soft dirt of the flower bed were small, petite.

Just about the size of Ellie's.

"Oh, no," Anna said to herself. She hurried inside, hesitating as she looked around the beautifully decorated cabin. She'd never suspected Ellie. Never.

She'd noticed a rolltop desk in an office, and she went to it. It was locked. In the kitchen Anna found a screwdriver and a hammer. Gritting her teeth, she forced the lock.

The manuscript pages were neatly stacked in the center of the desk. Anna felt as if she'd been punched. Her movements were cautious, almost as if she approached a snake, as she lifted the pages. Some of them showed red ink marks, notes made in the margin. She couldn't be positive that the writing was in Henry Mills's hand, yet she felt sure that it was.

Here was the sequel to *Blood on the Moon.*

Even more damning was the legal-size pages beside it. It took Anna only a moment to see that it was a contract for Blane Griffin's book. The contract lacked only Blane's signature. She remembered the message that had been left at the fire. Terms for a book contract for Blane had been written on the back—in what Jeremy thought was Blane's handwriting.

It took her a moment to find the figures for the book, but when she did, she pulled in a sharp breath. Blane had been offered a huge sum.

Standing in a pool of warm April sunshine, Anna held the pages, trying to piece the evidence together.

The connection between Blane and the murder was clear. But why would Ellie have the manuscript and contract? The manuscript had been at Jeremy's, except for the one page that had been left at the cave.

It took a couple of seconds for Anna to grasp the significance. When she did, she closed her eyes against the panic that threatened.

Ellie had had access to the knife. She had also known that Henry was alone at Jeremy's house. Anna forced herself to take a few deep breaths. She had the contract and the manuscript. No matter how guilty others looked, Ellie always seemed to turn up in the middle of things. Even to the point of finding Anna after Jeremy had disappeared and someone had stolen the key to the truck.

Anna knew she had no time to waste. That Ellie had betrayed her didn't shock her. It didn't even make her angry. So many things had been turned upside down in her life that she now accepted the unacceptable without a qualm.

She had accepted, too readily, that Jeremy had abandoned her. Yes, the facts had pointed to a scenario in which he had been picked up by a friend and had left, laughing at her gullibility. But she should have been the first to realize how facts and evidence could be twisted. And by Ellie!

She tried not to think about how Jeremy would take this news. She knew how much he valued the bookseller's friendship.

Now she was more determined than ever to find him. She should never have left the area where she'd last seen him. She realized now that she had been lured out of the wild Hill Country expressly so that Jeremy would be left alone, without assistance.

In the distance, the wailing sirens sounded like the cry of a lost baby. Anna darted around the side of the house in time to see the patrol cars flying toward the cabin.

Ellie had called the law! She'd probably made up some lie about how Anna had accosted her and how she'd escaped. The woman was capable of anything.

Anna sprinted to the river. The current was swift here, and the rocks treacherous. It wasn't a wide river or a deep one. But there was no safe crossing.

Which was exactly what Anna had hoped to find. Wading into the stream, she moved skillfully from rock to rock until she climbed out on the other side. Shaking the water from her feet, she hurried among the huge cypress trees that gave her plenty of cover— just as three sheriff's cars pulled into the drive of Ellie's house.

A deputy got out of one car and put a bullhorn up to his mouth.

"Anna Red Shoes, come out with your hands up. We know you're unarmed, and we don't want to hurt you. Come out now and save everyone a lot of trouble."

THE TRIP TO THE TRUCK was a burning hell of pain, but Jeremy made it, with Elissa Rivers's help. She talked to him the whole way. She told him of her life on the ranch that she now worked alone. She talked about the way the land had become her kin and family, and how the past and future had melded into the present for her—an old woman with only a short time left to live.

Judging by her strength and determination, Jeremy found it difficult to view Elissa as on the way out of life. She seemed to have a lot more vital force than he felt he had.

Ultimately, it was the talk that helped him make it to the old truck, and when Elissa pushed and prodded him into the seat, he collapsed without apology.

"Go on and pass out," she advised as she got in behind the steering wheel. "I've been giving it some thought, and I don't want to take you to the hospital, which is probably where you rightly belong. If we go there, you'll be in a heap of trouble, and likely so will I. I've got a friend…"

Jeremy tried to focus on what she was saying. It was all a slide of words that moved up and down and made no sense.

"Then it's decided," she said. "We'll go to my friend. It's a little unorthodox, and for a city man like you it's going to be strange, but since you've got a lot more to risk by getting caught than I do, we'll try to avoid the authorities."

Jeremy leaned back against the seat as the truck accelerated. His leg throbbed in a way that shut out almost all other thoughts. Except those of Anna.

Where was she? Was she okay?

He had to make it back to town to explain that she wasn't guilty of killing Henry.

"I need a phone." He was surprised when he said the words out loud.

"A phone?" Elissa repeated it as if she'd never heard the word before.

"I have to call, to make sure Anna isn't blamed."

The old woman nodded. "Yeah, I've been following the story. Seems you set out to capture the killer of your friend. What you're saying now is that you don't believe she's guilty. So you want to try to undo the damage that's been done.''

Everything she said sounded right to Jeremy, so he agreed.

''I don't know about a phone, but once I have you installed with Kee, I'll see about taking a message in to the sheriff for you. How about that?''

It was such an effort to concentrate on what she was saying. It would be so much simpler if he could just talk to Lem. ''No phone?''

''Gizmos are in short supply out where we're going. Why don't you write a note?'' She produced a scratch pad and a pencil from the glove box of the truck.

''I'll write Lem the truth,'' Jeremy agreed, taking the writing equipment.

''You concentrate on your note,'' Elissa said with a shake of her head. ''Just do what you do best, Mr. Writerman. Put it all down, and let's see if we can't put an end to some of the foolishness.''

Jeremy gripped the pencil and forced his mind to clear. He had to do this perfectly. He was a writer, and this time he was going to write the note that would clear Anna once and for all.

He took no notice of the fact that the truck headed northwest, deeper into the wilderness of the hills. He was still trying to write his note as the truck bumped off what little road there was and headed straight out across a flat that was so coated in trees that the shade was almost like dusk.

The rough trail was hard on his injured leg, making it pulse and throb with every bump. But he didn't think of that. He was only relieved to get out of the glare of the sun and the burning heat.

By the time Elissa stopped the truck in front of an

old cabin built of cedar trunks that hadn't been peeled, Jeremy was unconscious. He didn't hear her say that it was probably for the best. He didn't see the old man, about as frail and weathered as the woman, come out of the house and take a look at him.

"Blood poison," the man pronounced as he cut the leg of Jeremy's pants.

"Will he lose the leg?" Elissa asked.

"Depends on how hard he fights," the old man said. He picked up the notepad that Jeremy still held in his hand. After glancing at it, he looked up at Elissa. "Are you sure you want to be involved in this?"

"Too late to ask that question," she said, and laughed. "Brings to mind the old days, doesn't it?"

"Let's get him inside then."

Chapter Seventeen

"Hey, thanks, mister," Anna said as she got out of the car in downtown Kerrville and waved goodbye to the good Samaritan who'd given her a lift. She'd had no difficulty at all catching rides from Ellie's house into town.

It was odd, but even though her picture had been plastered all over the television as a potential murderer, no one seemed to recognize her. So much for notoriety, she thought as she took a position on a bench across from the sheriff's office.

She was in the heart of the enemy's camp, or at least that's the way Thunder Horse would view her position. She was determined to talk with the sheriff. Eventually. Anna knew it would look far better if she gave herself up rather than allowing them to capture her.

But before she did anything rash, she wanted to study the lay of the land.

And she wanted to see if there was news of Jeremy.

She'd taken the trouble to pull her hair back in a chignon, which didn't look too ridiculous with the slacks and silk blouse Ellie had loaned her. The slacks had suffered a little from the river, but they were dry now. Anna checked herself in the window of a café and saw, to her surprise, the image of a business-woman.

No wonder she wasn't being pinpointed as the murdering Native. She didn't look like a killer.

With that in mind, she decided to sit inside the café. She was starving, and some hot food and coffee would hit the spot. She also hoped to pick up on the local gossip.

The bell over the door jangled as she entered. For a moment she felt ten pairs of eyes swivel to examine her, and her heart pounded an alarm. Then everyone turned back to their conversations and food. It was only that she was a stranger in a place that had a lot of regulars.

Anna went to the counter and placed her order, sighing as hot coffee was placed in front of her. The little café was filled with talk, and she sipped her coffee and tried to sort out the conversations.

At a table to her left, four women were talking about the case. Anna's ears pricked up. One woman had heard the latest newscast in which the sheriff had gotten on television and pleaded with Jeremy to give himself up.

"That writer's long gone," another woman said. "He took off with that Native woman. They're probably somewhere on the other side of the world by now. I heard tell that all three of them were out on that ranch. The men were drinking and the dead man made a pass at the woman and then the writer killed him. There was a scene just like in one of his books, you know."

"Just goes to show, you never can tell," another woman said.

Anna hid her worried frown at the thought of such a foolish scenario, but the fact that such wild stories were circulating highlighted the seriousness of the situation. It was going to be harder than she'd anticipated to bring the rumor mill back under control, and to find the truth.

"Bad enough they killed the man—but then her leaving her friend in jail like that! And that woman risked a lot to help her. You'd think that she'd at least try to help her friend. Wouldn't a jailbreak be exciting?"

The coffee hit Anna's stomach with a bitter wallop. The only friend who could be in jail was Maria Gonzalez. Was it a fact, or just more of the gossipmongers' work? She wanted to grab the woman by the shoulders and shake the truth out of her, but she knew better. The worst thing she could do was to draw attention to herself.

The waitress set her hamburger in front of her, and Anna forced herself to eat. She needed the food, and she also needed a reason to sit at the counter and see what other tidbits she could pick up.

Lucinda Estar was another topic the foursome struck on. The women were divided—two admired Lucinda for riding with the posse and the other two thought she was a woman desperate for the limelight.

"Jeremy Masterson dumped her," an anti-Lucinda woman pointed out. "Now she's chasing him all over the country like she's the wrath of God. Honestly, it makes her look like some harridan from one of his books." There was a sharp intake of breath. "Do you think she could be Lorraine? Remember how Hank Chisholm was so in love with Lorraine? But toward the end of the book, I could sense that he was picking up on her true character.''

"I never thought of that," breathed another of the group. "But it makes sense. It fits perfectly, don't you think?''

Anna wanted to tell them that they were, finally, onto a bit of truth. Instead, she started eating her pile of French fries.

"Well, the posse is coming back this afternoon. They think Masterson and the woman made it to Mexico.''

"They're probably there right now, drinking tequila and living high off the hog.''

"Do you think someone will still publish his books? I mean, that movie director fellow moved to Europe when he was accused of statutory rape, and *he* still made a fortune directing.''

"I don't know. International laws are complicated. I say let them keep him.''

"But would you buy another of his books?''

There was general laughter as the women received their checks and got up. "Honey, I guess I have to admit that I would. I just love his writing.''

"You have no morals, Ginny," another woman laughed.

"But I have excellent literary taste.''

Giggling, they left the café.

Anna watched them exit—four women about her age, all going home to safe, sensible lives. What had happened to hers?

It was a question that required a lot of thinking, and she didn't have the time. The women have given her three very valuable pieces of information. Maria was in jail and the posse was coming in. Jeremy hadn't been captured, and he hadn't turned up in Kerrville.

So where was he?

She had a bad, bad feeling that he was injured and needing her. As she put the last French fry into her mouth, she fumbled in her slacks for cash. Lucky for her she always carried cash. Forty dollars wouldn't take her far, but it was all she had.

At the register she decided to risk a question. "Do you know where the sheriff keeps his posse horses?"

"There's a barn out Dewey Street. That's where they'll come in." The waitress checked her watch. "In fact, they should be there now." She turned to the kitchen. "Clara Belle, put on five more pots of coffee and get ready for some hungry men."

"They'll come here?"

"More than likely." The waitress stared up at her.

Anna felt panic, but she managed to control it. She didn't want the waitress to identify her, but she couldn't act strangely.

"Thanks," she said, heading for the door as quickly as she could without arousing suspicion.

Outside on the street, she knew she had a choice to make. Maria was in jail, and Jeremy was somewhere up in the rough country where she'd last seen him.

It wasn't a hard decision. Maria might be inconvenienced and angry, but Jeremy could die. She started walking toward the stables where the posse would unsaddle. It was insane. She was going to walk right into the midst of the people searching for her.

Twenty minutes later she was less than thirty yards from the stables, and well hidden in a stand of cottonwoods. To her delight, she saw her horse grazing in a small paddock. Allegro looked none the worse for her adventure.

The posse seemed worn and defeated as they gathered in a circle around the man Anna recognized as the sheriff. Lem was thanking them and telling them all to get rest and food. The trail was cold, but no one was giving up.

Anna wondered what the reaction would be if she simply walked up to him and gave herself up. That had been her original plan, until she'd become convinced that Jeremy needed her.

Lem was talking about justice and the need to continue the search, but she could see on the faces of the posse that a few days of playing cops and robbers had taken the shine off most of their badges.

There was only one—a tall, handsome man—who still had fire in his eyes. Blane Griffin. It had to be him. Anna watched as he paced, even though he was worn out. And he was joined by a tall, slender woman who took off her hat and allowed her beautiful red hair to cascade down her shoulders. Lucinda Estar. They spoke briefly—and angrily—from what Anna cold tell.

Shoulders stiff and back erect, Lucinda turned away from Blane and disappeared behind a big stock trailer. Anna caught sight of her again as she headed into the tree line behind the barn. Seconds later, a short, slender cowboy eased away from the crowd and began to follow her.

Watching them, Anna realized that it was a hint of furtiveness in their behavior that had caught her eye. Lucinda led the way far from the rest of the posse. The short cowboy walked right up to her, and Anna could tell by the stance and gesture that there was animosity between the two. In fact, the short cowboy pushed Lucinda.

To Anna's amazement, a third person stepped out from behind a truck.

Ellie!

Even from a distance Anna recognized her. Ellie stepped between Lucinda and the cowboy, clearly attempting to make peace.

The argument grew more heated, and Lucinda pushed the cowboy, who pushed her back. Then the short man turned abruptly and walked away. Ellie remained with Lucinda.

Anna cursed the fact that she was too far away to hear what had been said. She would have given plenty to know exactly how Lucinda was involved with Ellie.

But the short man had piqued her curiosity even more, so Anna decided to follow him. Learning his identity could save her hide—and Jeremy's.

JEREMY OPENED HIS EYES and then shut them again instantly. He couldn't believe what he saw. Hovering over him were an old woman and man, and they were wielding a knife that looked as if it could slice through bone.

"What do you think you're doing?" he asked, trying to move. It was only then that he realized he was tied down. "Hey!"

The old man turned to him, blood dripping off the knife. He glanced at the old woman. "He's a fighter, just like you said."

"Yeah, good stock. I guess I better head to town with that note, since he ain't gonna die."

"Where am I?" Jeremy asked. "What did you do to me?"

The old man finally addressed him, putting a hand on his forehead and pressing. "The fever is draining out of you with the poison. There was a pocket of infection in your wound. I lanced it, and now your leg will get better."

In honesty, Jeremy had to admit that it felt as if an intense internal pressure had been released in his leg. "Why am I tied up?"

"I had some antibiotics, for my cows. I used that, but I didn't have anything for pain. It was good that you were unconscious. I had to cut pretty deep."

"You used *cow* medicine?"

"Elissa says you write those books about Hank Chisholm. I read all of them. I love books. Remember when Gus got shot by the arrow in *Lonesome Dove?* If he'd had me to doctor him, he wouldn't have lost his leg."

Jeremy felt as if the Mad Hatter and the Queen of Hearts had captured him—but whatever they'd done, it was good medicine. "How long have I been here?"

"Six hours." Elissa grinned. "You're a strong man. You're comin' around fast."

"I have to get to town," Jeremy said. "There's a woman. She may be in danger."

Elissa held up the note. "You wrote this. I think it explains everything. I'll drive it in to town for you and see what I can do to find that woman."

"Anna. Her name is Anna Red Shoes."

"Granddaughter of Thunder Horse," Elissa said. "We have to talk about him."

"I know, I know," Jeremy said. "I'll make sure I get all of that straight. But Anna—"

"I'm goin'," Elissa said, shaking her head. "Men. Always in a hurry when it suits them." She stepped closer, her green eyes twinkling. "I told Kee that cow medicine would work on you."

Jeremy felt his bonds loosen as the old man untied him. He sat up and felt more strength than he had had in what seemed like days. "I want to go with you," he said.

Elissa shook her head. "No way. You stay here with Kee and let him tend you. You came mighty close to losing a leg."

Jeremy looked down at his limb. The marks made by the mountain lion were curved swirls. There was another, neatly stitched straight line, obviously the work of Kee.

"Are you a doctor?" he asked.

Kee laughed. "Veterinarian. Retired. Lucky I still keep some medicines out here for the range cows that get in trouble. A double bolus of cow medicine will kill any infection a man can harbor."

Jeremy nodded. "Lately I've been a very lucky man. But I get the feeling if I really want to stay lucky, I'd better get into town. I'm going with you, come hell or high water."

ANNA DIDN'T have to follow the cowboy far. The small man went to a green truck and began tossing his gear into the back. Anna was startled when he pulled his hat off and long, brunette hair tumbled down around his shoulders. Anna recognized Gabriel, the woman from the book signing.

Gabriel, too, could have had access to the knife. Anna was now at a point where she suspected everyone. But she also saw a golden opportunity. Gabriel was a small woman, and from the looks of her, not one who took pride in strength and skill. She'd also been talking with Ellie, which meant she knew something. Anna didn't hesitate. She snaked between the trucks and horse trailers until she was directly behind the brunette. Gabriel had already tossed her pistol into the cab of the truck. Anna waited until Gabriel moved around to the bed and began picking up halters and ropes. Then she darted forward, grabbed the gun and turned it on the woman.

"I'll shoot you. I don't have anything to lose," The fear in Gabriel's eyes told her that the woman believed she'd pull the trigger. Good. It was the edge Anna needed.

"Where's Jeremy?"

"Who do you think we've been looking for?" Gabriel said, tossing her hair back.

It was fine bravado, but Anna wasn't buying it. "I know you're involved with Ellie Clark. A man is dead, and Jeremy's seriously wounded. If he's out in those hills, he could die of infection. Now, I don't know what role you played in Henry Mills's murder, but I know for a fact you're involved in what's happened since then. You'll do at least ten years as an accomplice, and they won't be pretty years. You'll be, what, forty-five when you get out?"

Anna was fabricating and embellishing, but her words were having the desired effect.

"I didn't have a thing to do with this." Gabriel sounded desperate. "I didn't. Ellie knew I had a crush on Jeremy, and she told me to be at the bookstore. Then she told me to keep him busy at the party, and I did. That's all I knew about it. I didn't know somebody was going to get killed."

"Who did kill Henry Mills?" Anna wanted that hard fact.

"I don't know," Gabriel replied. Her voice was taut with fear. "I really don't. It could have been Blane or Ellie or Lucinda. Maybe all three of them. Lucinda and Ellie are crazy, and Blane doesn't care about anything but his book."

"And you?"

"I just wanted a chance at Jeremy. I knew he'd never even speak to me if he knew Lucinda and I were old college roommates. That's why I agreed to Ellie's plan. It seemed simple and harmless."

Gabriel was on the verge of tears, but Anna's pity was in short supply. She didn't believe or disbelieve Gabriel. She did, however, intend to scare the truth out of her—and then take it to the sheriff. Jeremy had to be found, and she was tired of lies and games.

"Why would Ellie want to kill Henry Mills?"

"Hell, why not blame the messenger?"

"And what exactly does that mean?" Anna cocked the gun. "Hurry up, Gabriel. I want answers and I don't have a lot of time."

"Ellie was furious with Henry because he offered Blane a huge contract."

Anna was still puzzled. "Keep talking. That doesn't make any sense."

"When Jeremy and Lucinda were having their little fling, Ellie and Blane got together. As soon as Jeremy dumped Lucinda, she went running back to Blane, and Ellie got left out." Gabriel sighed. "Ellie was furious. She'd helped Blane with his book. I mean, really helped him. She wanted him to be successful and she spent several months working with him—research, editing, all of it. She deserved co-authorship of that book."

"And he kicks her out and the book sells." Anna saw it clearly. "But why kill Henry?"

"I'm not certain she did it," Gabriel said. She held out her hands. "Look, I don't know anything. I really don't. You can't hold me accountable for this. I was only trying to get a date with Jeremy Masterson. I didn't know any of this was going to happen."

"But you didn't come forward."

Gabriel put her hands on her hips. "I didn't have anything to come forward with, except suspicions. And then you and Jeremy took off like scalded dogs. I thought maybe one of you *had* killed that editor. Why not? Jeremy could have been jealous of Blane's contract. It wouldn't be the first time. I know firsthand that close friends who turn into jealous enemies are the worst. Lucinda almost had a stroke when she heard I was with Jeremy. That's why she went to the party and made such an ass of herself. And all for what? He was only interested in finishing his book."

Anna had begun to believe the brunette. But she wasn't about to let her go. Gabriel was going to tell the sheriff everything she'd just said.

"I still don't see why Ellie would kill Henry." And she didn't.

"Maybe you should ask me?" Anna whirled around to find that Ellie Clark was directly behind her, the barrel of a gun only inches from her ribs.

"Put down the gun," Ellie said. "Now."

Anna had no choice but to comply.

"Hey! Hey! I've got Anna Red Shoes over here!" Ellie yelled. "Caught her red-handed, trying to kill Gabriel." Ellie glared over at the brunette. "You'd better start yelling for your life if you don't want to go to prison."

"Help!" Gabriel yelled weakly. "She was going to kill me."

Anna stared at her. "You know that isn't true."

"Louder!" Ellie commanded.

"Help!" Gabriel responded in a stronger voice. "Somebody come quick. This woman was going to kill me."

Anna felt as if she'd been snared in a spider web. Every time she tried to move, the web trembled and the spider drew closer and closer.

"Ellie," she said, "you can't get away with this. The truth is going to come out."

"I wouldn't bet on it. Without Jeremy to back up your story, all the evidence is against you. Not exactly the way I planned it, but there's nothing to do now but play out the cards."

"You should have left the area and gone home, Anna. But you had to hang around and go to Jeremy's house. I had it figured perfectly. Everyone was talking about your appearance at the store. Your knife—the murder weapon—I was going to say Blane took it from me at the party. To frame *you*. With all those witnesses knowing you'd left it at the store, no one would have believed him. It would have proven Blane's insane jealousy of Jeremy. Can't you see it? That would have been the icing on the cake, to put Blane in prison for the rest of his life. Premeditated murder. But you had to interfere. This is what you deserve."

Anna heard shouts and the sound of men hurrying toward them. Her impulse was to make a break for it, but she knew that Ellie would shoot her. She stood still and watched as the men arrived.

"Well, well, if it isn't the elusive Anna Red Shoes."

Anna looked squarely into the determined eyes of Blane Griffin.

Chapter Eighteen

The people crowded outside the sheriff's office seemed to multiply like bacteria. Every time Anna got a chance to look out the window, more and more had gathered. She was a celebrity—if one could call a criminal that.

They'd held her in a room alone. She'd asked to go back to the cells, hoping to find Maria. But so far, no one had honored that request, but she suspected it wouldn't be long before she found herself in a cell—after Lem had a chance to milk her arrest for all the media attention he could get.

She'd tried to talk to anyone who would listen about what she knew, but she was about to be booked for the murder of Henry Mills. The cameras and reporters were set up to capture the moment on film. She was beyond caring about her reputation. She was desperately worried about Jeremy. Lem believed that Jeremy had made it to Mexico, and no matter how Anna argued with him, he believed Ellie. Lying through her teeth, Ellie had insisted that she'd received a phone call from Jeremy saying he was safely across the border.

At the thought of Ellie, Anna wanted to leap across

the counter and force the truth out of her. She had to give up thoughts of physical aggression when the door opened and two deputies motioned her out.

Hands cuffed behind her, she was led to the main office. The glare of the television lights almost blinded her, and a dozen microphones were thrust in her face. The shouted questions of the reporters made little sense to her, but she had no intention of answering them, anyway.

"What's the charge, sheriff?" someone shouted.

"First-degree murder," Lem answered.

Anna couldn't restrain herself. "Jeremy said you were a fool," she said to Lem. "He said you couldn't investigate your way out of a paper bag."

"Well, I caught you," Lem said. "Along with my right-hand tracker here, Blane Griffin. He's one helluva writer, too, just about to become very famous."

Lem was clearly playing to the cameras, and Anna wanted to kick his shins. Just then, she saw a path opening through the reporters. She almost didn't believe her eyes, as an old woman elbowed her way up to the sheriff.

"I got somethin' for you," Elissa Rivers said to Lem. She held out a piece of white paper.

"Who are you?" the sheriff asked, arching one bushy eyebrow.

"Oh, just an old woman. You'll want this, though." She thrust the paper into his hand. "Read it out loud."

Lem unfolded the paper. He scanned it and a deep frown cut ridges between his eyebrows. He cleared his throat and began to read. "I was left in the hills to die from infection. The only person who tried to help me was Anna Red Shoes. She didn't kill Henry. If you want to get to the bottom of this, meet me outside."

Lem's voice had dropped with each successive sentence. Finally, looking into the cameras, he concluded, "It's signed by Jeremy Masterson."

There was a momentary hush in the room, then all hell broke loose. Anna was abandoned. Lem turned to Blane, who'd been standing against the wall. Blane hurried forward and took the note. He examined it. "Looks like Jeremy's writing," he said.

"Well, you want to get him, he's outside waiting for you," the old woman said. A sly grin touched her face. "But you need to bring her—" She pointed at Anna. "I won't take you to him without her."

"She's a suspect in a murder," Lem said.

"Oh, quit being such a perfect jackass," Elissa said with a snap. "You're already going to look like an idiot on the television. Don't make it worse. Take those dang cuffs off her, and let's make some tracks."

Lem walked up behind Anna and unlocked the cuffs. "Don't try anything."

Anna shook her wrists, turned and glared up at the sheriff. "You have Maria Gonzalez in jail. What are the charges?"

"Aiding and abetting a wanted criminal."

Before Anna could say anything, Elissa Rivers spoke up. "Looks to me like you'd better let her go, sheriff. If this one here ain't guilty, then the other one didn't aid and abet no criminal."

To Anna's surprise, Blane touched the sheriff's shoulder. "Look, if Jeremy is out there injured, the important thing is getting him to a hospital. Cut her loose. If we need her, I promise you I'll get her back."

Anna saw the honest worry in his eyes. No matter how angry Blane and Jeremy were, there was a long history between them, and a lot of positive emotion.

"Get her," Lem said, tossing the keys to a deputy. "Now let's go."

JEREMY SAT UNDER the shade of an oak and watched the horde of reporters disgorged from the courthouse. Elissa had done her job well. Sitting beside him, Kee didn't offer an opinion. They watched in silence as Elissa led Lem and Blane and the reporters straight to him.

The one thing Jeremy hadn't expected was Anna in the lead.

"Anna!" He stood up despite his bad leg and Kee's restraining hand. Anna didn't wait. She rushed into his arms with a cry of delight that did more to heal him than any medicine he could have taken.

He crushed her to him, burying his face in her silky hair.

She pushed back, her gaze holding his as she searched his face. "You're okay. Elissa said they had to operate on you."

"And a damn fine job of it they did." He turned to Kee. "This is Anna Red Shoes."

Anna froze. She stepped out of Jeremy's arms and went up to the old man, hugging him close to her. "I thought you were dead."

"Not quite," he said, chuckling. "I gave up my practice and moved to a place of solitude."

"You know him?" Jeremy interrupted.

"Remember the great healer I told you about? This is his son, Standing Owl."

"But he said his name was Kee."

Anna laughed. "*Kee* is the sound a bird makes when it's soaring high. It's a joke."

Jeremy could only put his arm around Anna and hug

her against him. "I see you brought the posse with you."

"No choice. They were going to lynch me," she said. "Elissa and your note turned the tide."

Jeremy couldn't keep his hands off Anna. He grasped her shoulders, making sure she was solid and not injured. He ignored the others until Blane spoke out.

"You've got a lot of explaining to do," Blane said. "I suggest, since you're able to stand, you start talking."

"Blane was the only one who'd listen to me," Anna said. "We need his help. This involves him."

"Don't I know it," Jeremy said sarcastically as he glared at his old friend.

"Not like you think. He's as much a victim as we've been."

"Right." Jeremy wasn't inclined to sympathize with the man who'd pursued him.

Anna grasped his arm, pressing deep with her fingers. "Just listen to what I say to them, then make your decisions. Promise?"

"I promise." He would have agreed to fly if it meant keeping her by his side. Whatever else happened, he was not going to let this woman get away.

She helped him over to a seat, then stepped back and allowed Lem to begin his questioning.

"Ellie said you were in Mexico," the sheriff said, aware that television cameras were recording every second. He waved at them to go away, but they ignored him.

"Ellie said that?" Jeremy looked around, and when he failed to see her he turned to Anna. He saw the sorrow and worry on her face. It was the only clue he needed. "What else did she say?"

"That you'd confessed your guilt and that this woman here had helped you commit the murder. She said that Henry had rejected your latest book and—"

"That's ridiculous. The manuscript was on my desk. He was editing it. We'd already agreed on the advance. The publisher wouldn't bother to send an editor all the way down here to reject a book!"

He felt Anna's hand on his leg, soothing him. He took a long breath.

Lem shook his head. "There wasn't a manuscript on the desk at all. Nothing was there, and the computer was empty. Nothing."

"Lem, can you even turn a computer on?" Jeremy asked in frustration. His book had to be on that computer. It had to.

"The manuscript is in Ellie's desk," Anna said quietly, "except for the page of it she left for us up in the hills. And so is the contract for Blane's book."

Lem turned to her. "You're making this up!"

"You know I was in her cabin. She lured me there, telling me not to give myself up. Then she called you to snare me. I saw the manuscript and contract when I was there. That's why I ran."

Lem's eyes narrowed. "Why would Ellie do this?"

"For Blane," Anna said softly. She tightened her hold on Jeremy's knee. "She was in love with Blane."

"That's ridicu—" Blane halted halfway, a series of memories playing through his mind and clearly reflected in his features. "She never loved me. She told me point-blank that our affair was only a fling for her. And why would she kill Henry?"

Jeremy understood. "Because he'd accepted your

new book. He told me he was excited about it, Blane. He said it was the best work you'd ever done. It was supposed to be a secret, though.''

''That's right. It was going to be a secret until the manuscript was polished.'' Blane bit at the corner of his bottom lip. ''I knew Ellie was mad at me when I started seeing Lucinda again, but this is crazy. To kill a man because he was helping my career!''

''It was more than that,'' Anna said.

Jeremy could tell how much she hated to continue. For all she'd been through, for all of the false accusations that had been hurled at her, she took no pleasure in seeing others hurt. He put his arm around her shoulders and gave a squeeze. ''Go on,'' he urged.

''She was going to frame you for the murder, Blane. She wanted to ruin you. It was too much for her that you'd gone back to Lucinda and then sold the book that she'd helped you with.''

''She helped, but—'' Blane looked at Jeremy. ''She did help me, but in the same way she said she helped you. I never thought—'' He paused.

''It was a perfect setup,'' Anna added. ''but then I got in the way and messed things up. And Jeremy, too.''

''Holy cow,'' Lem said. ''I'd better get on the radio right now. I talked to her not half an hour ago. I'll have some deputies pick her up before she can get too far.''

ANNA, JEREMY AND MARIA sat under the awning of the small café and watched as Ellie and Gabriel were led up the courthouse steps. The throng of reporters had grown.

''We'd better be on our way,'' Jeremy said. ''Once

they spot us, they'll be after us like hounds on a rabbit.''

"It won't take them long to find Johnny, either," Maria said. "I can't believe he left you to die, Jeremy. But at least he told Elissa where you were."

"Anna and I both will talk with Lem about the charges against him," said Jeremy. "I don't want to prosecute. I don't think he meant to nearly kill us when he shot out the tire."

"Legally, he may be okay. Morally, that's another issue. He can buy me out or I'll buy him out. I won't be in business with him. He left you out there injured, knowing you could die," Maria said. "Whatever his reasons, they aren't good enough. I don't need someone like him in my life."

Anna wanted to comfort her friend, but there was nothing she could say. Johnny *was* a cad, and Maria was better off without him.

"Uh-oh, here comes trouble."

At the sound of Jeremy's tone, Anna looked up. Lucinda Estar was walking toward them, her stride long and purposeful.

"I hope you're happy now," she said angrily. "Blane has told me to pack my things and get out. How did he find out that I suggested the idea of the reward to your publisher? All I did was pump your book sales."

"I had nothing to do with it," Jeremy said. "Nothing."

"You got a million dollars' worth of free publicity for your book, you're a household name—and I got dumped."

"Oh, did I forget to thank you?" Jeremy asked. "What an oversight on my part. You had half the county out trying to kill me and bring in my hide for a bounty. How can I *ever* thank you?''

''Just quit whining. You sound just like Blane. Now that the two of you have patched up your friendship and he's going to be a big-time writer, he doesn't need me. The two of you can just ride off into the sunset together.'' She glared at Anna. ''Maybe they'll let you go along to cook and clean for them. You deserve Jeremy.'' She turned on her heel and left.

''A black pit of unhappiness,'' Maria said.

The comment struck Anna as funny, and once she started laughing, she couldn't stop. Jeremy joined her, and soon all three were lost in their mirth.

Finally Anna got her breath. When she looked up into Jeremy's eyes, she saw the humor, and something much deeper. She was transfixed by the passion and promise in his eyes.

''Hey!'' Maria said. ''If you two are going to stand on the street mooning over each other, I'd better head home. Thanks for the loan of the truck, Jeremy. I'll get it back to you.''

''No problem,'' Jeremy said, his full attention on Anna.

''I'll be by in a day or two,'' Anna said. ''I have to start to put my life back together.''

''I'll see you when I see you,'' Maria called back as she hurried toward the parking lot.

Anna continued to stare into Jeremy's eyes. There were questions there, but also answers. And so much more. Not so long ago she'd looked into a mirror and seen some of those same emotions. Hope, doubt, fear…and love for a man she wasn't certain she could trust. Now she knew she could trust him, with her heart, and with her life.

"What are you planning on doing?" Jeremy asked softly.

"I don't know if I have a job. I don't know anything," Anna replied. For some reason, though, she wasn't worried.

"Would you consider working for me?"

"Pardon?" Of all the questions he might have asked, this wasn't the one she expected.

"I'm working on a book about Texas and the early years. There's this intriguing figure—a Native American leader named Thunder Horse. I thought you might want to help me with the research."

"Really?" Anna couldn't hide her joy. Jeremy was going to keep his word. He was going to vindicate her grandfather.

"There's one condition."

She felt a tiny wound to her joy. "What?"

He picked up her hand, bringing it slowly to his lips. He kissed each finger, then returned to her third. "You have to wear a particular ring on this finger." He turned her hand over and kissed her palm, his lips sending a flood of sensation through her. "My ring."

Anna felt her heart pounding.

"Marry me, Anna. Be my partner. In my writing and in my life."

Anna felt the tears welling in her eyes. Tears! At the moment of her greatest happiness, she was going to cry.

"Anna?" Jeremy's face suddenly folded into worry. "Are you okay?"

"Damnation," she said, wiping at the tears. "After everything we've gone through together, you finally made me cry."

His arms came around her and she felt as if she'd

found the haven she'd been seeking most of her life. "I'll marry you, Jeremy," she said. "I'll be your wife and make sure your research, at least about Thunder Horse, is accurate."

She felt his arms tighten.

"I'll make you happy," he whispered. "Whatever it takes, Anna, that's what I'll do."

"Then just be who and what you are—Jeremy Masterson, descendant of a famous lawman. And I'll be the granddaughter of Thunder Horse. Together we can forge a future, for ourselves and our children."

Looking For More Romance?

Visit Romance.net

Check in daily for these and other exciting features:

Hot off the press

View all current titles, and purchase them on-line.

What do the stars have in store for you?

Horoscope

Hot deals

Exclusive offers available only at Romance.net

Plus, don't miss our interactive quizzes, contests and bonus gifts.

PWEB

CHRISTIANE HEGGAN

"A master at creating taut,
romantic suspense."
—*Literary Times*

ENEMY WITHIN

When Rachel Spaulding inherits her family's Napa Valley
vineyard, it's a dream come true for the adopted daughter of
loving parents. But her bitter sister, Annie, vows to do
whatever it takes to discredit Rachel and claim the Spaulding
vineyards for herself. Including digging into Rachel's past.

What she digs up uncovers three decades of deceit. And
exposes Rachel to a killer who wants to keep the past buried.

On sale mid-February 2000 wherever paperbacks are sold!

MIRA

Amnesia…an unknown danger…
a burning desire.

With

HARLEQUIN®

I N T R I G U E ®

you're just

A MEMORY AWAY…

from passion, danger…and love!

**Look for all the books in this
exciting miniseries:**

A NIGHT WITHOUT END (#552)
by Susan Kearney
On sale January 2000

FORGOTTEN LULLABY (#556)
by Rita Herron
On sale February 2000

HERS TO REMEMBER (#560)
by Karen Lawton Barrett
On sale March 2000

A MEMORY AWAY…where remembering
the truth becomes a matter of life,
death…and love!

HARLEQUIN®
Makes any time special ™

Come escape with Harlequin's new

Series Sampler

Four great full-length Harlequin novels bound together in one fabulous volume and at an unbelievable price.

Be transported back
in time with a
Harlequin Historical®
novel, get caught up
in a mystery with Intrigue®,
be tempted by a hot, sizzling romance
with Harlequin Temptation®,
or just enjoy a down-home
all-American read with
American Romance®.

You won't be able to put this collection down!

On sale February 2000 at your favorite retail outlet.

HARLEQUIN®
Makes any time special ™

Visit us at www.romance.net   PHESC